* * * * * * *

As the days passed, the small band of adventurers continued to move west making only ten to twelve miles a day. The conditions seemed to get worse with each passing day and each passing mile. Water had to be rationed, and buffalo dung had to be gathered wherever it could be found to use in place of firewood. The heat of the day and the dust blowing almost constantly made some of the members of the small band lose sight of their goals, and some of them to lose their faith while some of them simply lost hope.

But those were not the only problems that they would face. There were many dangers in crossing the plains. One of the many dangers they faced showed up just two weeks after crossing the Missouri River.

* * * * * * *

Other Large Print Editions by J.E. Terrall

Western Short Stories
  The Old West
  The Frontier
  Untamed Land
  Frontier Justice
  Tales from the Territory

Western Novels

  Conflict in Elkhorn Valley
  The Valley Ranch War

TALES FROM THE TERRITORY

A COLLECTION OF SOUTH DAKOTA WESTERN SHORT STORIES

by

J.E. Terrall

ISBN: 978-0-9994727-2-9

This is a work of fiction. Names, characters, and incidents are either a product of the author's imagination or are used fictitiously, and any resemblance to actual persons, living or dead, is purely coincidental.

Printed in the United States of America

Large print edition printed by creatspace.com

Cover: Front and back cover photos taken by author, J.E Terrall

Book Layout/
Formatting: J.E. Terrall
        Custer, South Dakota

TALES FROM THE TERRITORY

A COLLECTION OF SOUTH DAKOTA WESTERN SHORT STORIES

To
Gracie R. Terrall,
my granddaughter and fellow author,
with love.

TALES FROM THE TERRITROY

THE CHRISTMAS VISITOR

The place was the Dakota Territory east of the Black Hills and a little north of the Bad Lands. The year was 1869, the date was December, fourth, and the weather could only be described as horrible. The wind blew out of the north and had been for the past two days. The snow swirled around with a vengeance making it difficult to see more than a few feet. It was the kind of weather that was not fit for man nor beast. It was no time to be outside.

Bessie McDonald was sitting in her rocking chair by the fire knitting a sweater. Her young son, Billy, was lying in his bed in the loft that overlooked the one room of the small but cozy cabin. Bessie often looked at the small picture of her husband on the mantel above the fireplace. It had been five long and lonely months since she had buried him.

For the first couple of years that Bessie and her husband had lived on the prairie, they had struggled to raise a garden and a few head of cattle. The hard winters, along with hot, dry summers, had made it difficult. Just when it was beginning to look like they might make a go of it, her husband got sick and died.

Bessie had thought about going back to Georgia to find a position as a school teacher. It was a position that she had held when the Civil War broke out. By the time Bessie was emotionally ready to think about what to do, it was too late in the fall to go back east.

She thought that it would be better for them to stay one more winter than to try to move to Georgia with winter coming on. If they stayed, they would have enough to eat to get them through the winter. The garden had produced a good crop which Bessie had canned. There were plenty of animals, both large and small, in the area they could hunt to put meat on the table.

Thoughts of loneliness crept into Bessie's mind as tears slowly welled up in her eyes. She missed the companionship and love of her husband. She reached up and wiped the tears from her eyes, then scolded herself for letting her seclusion get the better of her emotions.

She had a son to look after, and he was the most important person in her life. In fact, he was the only person in her life.

Billy was only nine years old and no longer had a father to help him grow up. He was able to do some of the chores, but he was not big enough, or strong enough, to do many of the tasks it took to run even a small farm. Bessie worried about him growing up without a father. A boy needed a man in his life.

Her thoughts were disturbed by a noise at the door. She looked at the door and listened. The only thing she could hear was the wind as it blew against the cabin. She turned back to her knitting, but was again disturbed by the noise.

Bessie stared at the door as she put her knitting down. She stood up and wrapped a shawl around her shoulders, then walked to the door and listened. It was a minute or so before she heard the sound again. It was a strange sound, almost as if someone or something was scratching the ground in front of the door.

Pulling her shawl tightly around her shoulders, she picked up the pistol she kept on a shelf next to the door. Gripping the gun in both hands, she cocked it. She then reached out with one hand and released the catch on the door. Slowly, she opened the door then quickly stepped back, almost falling over a bench by the table.

She was surprised to see a large brown and white horse standing in front of the door. The horse had a saddle, a bridle and a rifle in the scabbard. There were also a bedroll and saddlebags on the horse, but no rider. The horse stood looking at her, then began bobbing its head up and down.

Afraid that someone might be lurking outside, Bessie tried to look around the horse. When she didn't see anyone, she moved closer to the door again. She still couldn't see anyone, or any tracks that would indicate someone was out there.

Since the horse seemed nervous, she slowly reached out and took hold of the reins with her free hand. The horse stepped back a little, but made no effort to try to get away from her.

The horse pranced a little from side to side. When it turned sideways, Bessie noticed that there was blood on the saddle. She looked around for someone who might be hurt, but couldn't see very far in the blowing snow and darkness. Her only light was from the light reaching out into the darkness from inside the cabin.

She led the horse to the hitching post to the right of the door and tied it there. Bessie went back inside and put on a coat, then grabbed the lantern from the shelf next to the door. She held it up in the hope of seeing what might be out there. She thought she could see something dark lying in the snow about twelve feet from the cabin.

In the dark, she couldn't make out what it was. She slowly moved closer to the dark object. She discovered that it was a dark coat lying in the snow. Bessie tucked the gun in her apron as she approached the coat. She bent down and lifted the coat up. There was a man lying under it. At first she wasn't sure if he was alive, but when she touched the side of his face, he groaned.

His groan startled her causing her to jump back, but she quickly regained her composure. The man was injured and needed help, and he needed it now.

Bessie ran back to the cabin and set the lantern and her gun on the shelf next to the door. Returning to the injured man, she rolled him over on his back. When his coat fell open, she could see a large dark area on the left side of his shirt. She was sure it was blood. She also noticed the silver star of a Territorial Marshal pinned to his shirt.

She moved to his head, grabbed his coat and pulled him across the snow toward the cabin. It took all the strength that she could muster to get him into the cabin.

Once he was inside, she shut the door and bolted it. She called Billy to help her as she stripped the marshal of his coat and gun, and then took off his boots. With Billy's help, she put him on her bed. When Bessie took his shirt off and removed the bandana that was covering the wound, she found that he had been shot on his left side. When she turned him over, she could see that the bullet had passed through him.

Bessie heated some water, then cleaned and dressed his wound. She tied a long piece of soft cloth around him tightly to keep his wound covered, and to keep pressure on the wound to stop the bleeding. After she finished dressing his wound, she covered him with a quilt and put an extra log on the fire to warm the cabin.

As soon as she had done all she could for him, she looked at her son. He was watching her.

"We will just have to wait to see if he will live. Keep an eye on him. I'll be right back."

"Where ya goin'?"

"It's 'where are you going'," she reminded him. "I'm going to take care of his horse. I'll be back in a few minutes."

Bessie put on her coat and went outside to take care of the marshal's horse. She led the horse into the barn, put it in a stall, then took off the saddle. After wiping the horse down with a rag, she fed it then returned to the cabin with the marshal's rifle and saddlebags.

When she entered the cabin, she saw her son sitting next to the bed watching the marshal. He had a worried look on his face.

"Will he be all right?" Billy asked as he looked at his mother for an answer.

"I don't know, but we've done all we can for now. You might as well go back to bed."

Bessie gave him a kiss on the cheek, then watched him as he climbed up to the loft. She knew that he would not go right to sleep. As soon as her son had settled down in the loft, she busied herself with taking care of the marshal's clothes.

It was only after she had done as much for him as she could that she had a chance to think about what he was doing out in the storm, and why he had been shot. Her mind filled with questions she knew would not get answered until he came around.

She sat down in her chair, covered herself with a quilt and watched him. She was exhausted; but with a stranger, even a marshal, in the cabin, she found it difficult to go to sleep. She sat watching him for what seemed like hours. He never moved. She could only hope that he would survive.

As the night wore on, Bessie dozed off and on. Waking up from time to time, she looked at the marshal. He seemed to be mumbling in his sleep, but she could not understand him.

When morning finally came, Bessie woke and looked at the marshal. His color had improved a little which gave her hope that he would survive. She stood up, folded the quilt and placed it on the back of the chair. When she turned back around to check on the marshal, she was surprised to see his eyes open. He was watching her.

"How are you feeling, Marshal?"

"Am I still alive, or are you an angel?"

"You are still alive," she replied with a smile.

"In that case, I need to get out of here."

"You can't go anywhere. You'll start bleeding again."

"I have to go," he insisted.

"If you go out in the storm, you will die," Bessie insisted. "Besides, you wouldn't get as far as the barn."

The marshal laid there and looked at her. He could feel the pain in his side and was sure she was right. A glance toward the window showed him it was still snowing and blowing. If it had been snowing all night, his tracks would have been wiped away. With that thought in mind, he closed his eyes and dozed off.

Bessie wanted the answers to a dozen or more questions. The most important one was what made him risk his life traveling in a storm. She didn't try to talk to him then. He needed to rest.

Bessie was cooking lunch when she glanced over at the bed. The marshal was watching her again. It made her feel a little self-conscious, especially after he had wanted to know if she was an angel.

"Well, I see you are awake. Are you hungry?"

"Yes, ma'am."

"I'll fix you some broth."

"Thank you," he said then closed his eyes.

The marshal didn't go back to sleep. Instead he was thinking about the woman and her son, and about the fact he could not protect them if trouble came. He could only hope that he didn't bring his troubles into their home.

It wasn't long before Bessie had a bowl of broth ready for him. She moved over to the bed and sat down in a chair beside it.

"Are you ready to try to eat something?" she asked in a soft voice.

He opened his eyes and looked up at her. He couldn't help but think how pretty she looked and how caring she was being to him.

"Yes, ma'am."

"Let me help you sit up."

Bessie stood up, then leaned down over him and pulled him up. He watched her as she tucked a couple of pillows behind his head.

"Are you comfortable?" she asked as she looked down at him.

"Yes, ma'am," he said as he looked into her blue eyes.

"I'll help you."

She sat down and began feeding him. She noticed him watching her which made her feel uncomfortable. It had been a long time since a man had looked at her that way.

When he was finished, she took the bowl over to the counter. When she turned around, she found him still watching her.

"Is there something else you need," she asked.

"I was just wondering why such a beautiful woman as you is here alone."

"I am not alone. I have my son with me."

"But there is no man around. Why is that?"

Bessie looked at him. She wasn't sure that she wanted to answer him, but having an adult to talk to for the first time in a long time might help relieve at least some of her loneliness.

"My husband died almost six months ago. I decided it was too late in the fall for us to leave."

"So it's just you and the boy?"

"Yes, but we are quite able to take care of ourselves," she said with a hint of strength in her voice.

"I have no doubt. I am very glad you are here. If you had not been, I would have died less than twenty feet from the shelter of your home. For that, I am forever indebted to you."

Bessie did not know what to say to him. It embarrassed her to think that he felt indebted to her. She had only done what she felt anyone would do under the circumstances.

"May I ask you a couple of questions?" Bessie asked.

"Sure."

"What is your name?"

"My name is Sam Briggs. I'm the Territorial Marshal."

"What were you doing out in such a storm?"

"It's kind of a long story, but since you saved my life I think you should know. I was following a man who was wanted for murdering and robbing a family over near the Missouri River. I caught up with him at a small trading post. He was drunk and mean. I tried to avoid an argument with him, but he was determined to get into a gunfight. When I tried to arrest him, he went for his gun. I had no choice but to defend myself. He drew on me and I had to kill him."

"He apparently shot you, too. What was the name of the man you were after?"

"The man's name was Jessie Morgan. It turned out that he has several brothers, three in fact. They are all wanted and have a price on their heads. They caught me in the trading post, and I had to fight my way out. It was one of Jessie's brothers who shot me. Since I was wounded, I got out of there. I knew I could always go back and get them later, once my injury healed."

"Why did you head out this way? Wouldn't it have been better to go east?"

"They cut off my way east. They didn't even take time to bury the one I had shot. They've been dogging my heels ever since. When it started to snow, I figured that I might lose them if I kept going. I think they held up somewhere because of the storm. Hopefully, they lost my trail."

"How far is it from here to where you were shot?"

"I'm not sure. When did you find me?"

"Yesterday evening."

"I think I was shot two days before you found me."

"The storm started late that same day," Bessie said as she looked at him.

"That would be right. It had just started to snow. I got lost in it."

"I'm sure they will have a hard time finding you, now."

"I hope so."

* * * *

The storm ended and the days turned warm enough that some of the snow melted. As the days passed, the marshal's wounds healed and he grew stronger. As soon as he was able to get around, he did what he could to help out. He spent most of his time helping Billy with some of the chores in order to help regain his strength. He found Billy to be a hard worker even though there were many things he would not be able to do by himself until he was older and stronger. Together, they managed to get them done.

All the time Sam was with Billy and his mother, he kept an eye out for the Morgan brothers. The one thing he noticed was there were very few people who came anywhere close to the farm, but that was to be expected. There were very few settlers in the area. It could be as much as thirty to forty miles, or more to the nearest neighbor.

It slowly grew colder as Christmas came closer. It would snow a little bit from time to time, but not more than an inch or so at a time. The snow didn't show any tracks that would tell Sam there was anyone else around.

When it was less than a week before Christmas, Sam was starting to feel much better. It was getting close to the time when he should be moving on.

Billy was talking about getting a Christmas tree, and told Sam where they might find one. Sam agreed to help Billy get a tree. When they had their horses ready, Sam told Billy to lead the way. They rode off toward the river over a mile away from the cabin to see if they could find a tree.

Sure enough, they found a little pine tree that would make the perfect Christmas tree for the small cabin. They cut it down and tied it across Billy's saddle. Billy rode behind Sam as they headed back to the cabin.

When they were about one hundred yards from the cabin, Sam noticed fresh tracks from three horses in the snow. He stopped, stepped out of the saddle and knelt down to study the tracks. They were the tracks of three shod horses, which meant they were white men's horses.

There was little doubt in Sam's mind that the tracks had been made by the horses of the Morgan brothers. He looked off in the direction the tracks had gone. It was obvious they were headed toward the cabin. Since it had not snowed that day, they were sure to find the tracks left by Billy and Sam's horses around and near the barn.

"We have to be very careful. These tracks might be from the three men who are after me."

"What do we do? My mother is all alone," Billy said with a worried look on his face.

"We'll leave the horses here. We'll go on foot the rest of the way. Billy, do you know how to use a rifle?"

"Sure. My dad taught me how to shoot. I've been hunting for over a year," he said proudly.

"Good. I want you to take my rifle and keep me covered. Don't shoot unless you have to, and make sure of what you are shooting at," Sam said as he took his rifle from his saddle scabbard.

"Okay," Billy said as he took the rifle from Sam.

"See that little rise over there? It runs around behind the barn."

"Yeah."

"I want you to go to the back side of the ridge and work your way around behind the barn. You should be able to see the front of the cabin from the corner. Keep a close watch."

"Okay."

As soon as Billy had disappeared behind the ridge, Sam headed for the ravine that ran close to the cabin. Moving along the bottom of the ravine as fast as his wound would let him, Sam was able to get very close. When he was only about twenty feet from the front of the cabin, he leaned against the side of the ravine and looked over the edge.

He could see all three of the Morgan brothers. James and Jacob were sitting on their horses. They were facing the cabin. The third and oldest, Frank Morgan, was standing on the ground in front of his horse facing the cabin. Sam could not see in the cabin, but it was clear that Frank was talking to Bessie. He was close enough to hear them.

"Excuse me, ma'am, but we're lookin' for a man who rides a brown and white paint."

"There's no one here who rides a horse like that."

"We've been trackin' that horse for a long time. Ma'am, we done seen its tracks just the other side of your barn. So we know you're lyin'."

"Oh. We have a horse that might look like the one you described, but it is my husband's horse."

"How did he come 'bout gettin' the horse?"

"Some gentleman rode in here on the horse during a storm. He was almost dead when we found him. Someone had shot him. We tried to save him, but it was too late. Before he passed on, he asked my husband to take good care of his horse."

Frank turned and looked up at his brothers. He wasn't sure if the woman was telling the truth or not. He turned back and looked at the woman again.

"Where's your husband now?"

"He is out getting a Christmas tree with our son."

"When will he be back?"

"I'm not sure. It could be almost dark before they get back. They have to go a long ways to get a good Christmas tree," Bessie said with a smile.

"I'm sure they do," Frank said politely, but he was still not sure she was telling him the truth.

Frank stood there for a few minutes trying to figure out what to do next. He was almost sure she was lying to him, but there was a possibility that she was telling him the truth. Frank knew he had shot the marshal when he tried to get away after killing his younger brother. Frank also knew there had been a nasty snowstorm, and the marshal had continued into the storm. The storm had been so severe it held Frank and his brothers up for several days. They lost his trail and had spent over two weeks trying to find it. It was only by chance they had found the tracks of his horse there.

"I think we'll just wait," Frank said. "And I think we'll wait in the cabin where it's warmer."

"I don't think you will. I do not open my home to strangers, especially armed strangers who are hunting a marshal," she said.

"I will not give up my guns to any woman. I will go into any cabin I want, with or without a woman's permission," he said as he put his hand on the pistol at his side.

"This pistol gives me all the authority I need to stop you," Sam called out from the ravine. "And the rifle pointed at you from the barn backs it up."

"Well, I see you're still alive, Marshal," Frank said.

Suddenly, James went for his gun. Sam saw him and shot him out of the saddle. At the same time there was a rifle shot fired from the corner of the barn. The shot hit right in front of Jacob's horse causing the horse to jump and buck, dumping Jacob on the ground.

Frank quickly realized that the marshal was not alone. He put his hands out to his sides and stood very still hoping they would not shoot him.

"Very carefully, drop your gun belt," Sam said.

Frank had a disgusted look on his face. He had been caught and there was nothing he could do but surrender. He unbuckled his gun belt and let it drop to the ground.

Sam was keeping a close eye on Frank. Suddenly Jacob tried for his gun. Sam caught the movement out of the corner of his eye and instantly turned and fired at Jacob. The shot hit Jacob in the center of his chest, killing him instantly.

Frank tried to take advantage of the moment and dove for his gun. He had just grabbed it when a shot was fired from inside the cabin. The shot hit him in the leg. Frank turned and pointed his gun toward the front of the cabin when two more shots were fired, one from a pistol and one from a rifle. Both shots hit Frank, killing him.

When the shooting was over, Billy came out from behind the corner of the barn. He walked toward the cabin, all the time keeping his gun pointed at the men lying on the ground.

Bessie came out of the cabin with a gun in her hand. She ran to her son, took him in her arms and held him tightly.

Sam came out of the ravine and walked up to the others. He looked from the three dead men on the ground to Bessie and Billy.

"Why don't you take Billy inside? I'll take care of them," Sam said.

Bessie looked up at him. She wanted to say something to him, but didn't know what to say at the moment. She nodded, then turned and took Billy into the cabin.

As soon as Billy and his mother were inside the cabin, Sam started gathering up the guns and gun belts of the Morgan brothers and put them on a bench by the door to the cabin. He got a team of horses from the barn and hitched them to the wagon, then put the bodies in the wagon along with a shovel. He took the bodies away from the cabin.

Sam found a place along the ravine where there was a good sized overhang of dirt above a curve in the ravine. There were a lot of rocks scattered around the area, too. Sam buried the Morgan brothers in the ravine and covered the graves with rocks. He caved the overhang of dirt over the graves and put more rocks over it, then returned to the barn. He unhitched the team of horses and took care of them. He also retrieved the Christmas tree and the horses he and Billy had been riding. After taking care of all the horses, he went and knocked on the door of the cabin. Bessie answered the door.

"I've taken care of the Morgan brothers. I put their horses in the barn. You might as well have them since they no longer have a need for them. I also brought the Christmas tree that Billy and I got for you."

"Won't you please come in," Bessie said.

"Are you sure?"

"Yes. We don't have much, but we would like you to spend Christmas with us. Unless you have somewhere else you have to be for Christmas."

"I have no place else that I have to be," he said with a smile.

The three of them set up the Christmas tree and decorated it with stars and angels made from paper. They also wrapped strings of popcorn around the tree. It was clear that Bessie and Billy had very little, but were willing to share what they had with him.

There was no talk of the three men who had died there. They all knew that it was a hard land they had chosen to live on, and they had to defend themselves in any way they could. It was not the first time that Bessie, her husband and son had to fight to keep their small farm. An occasional small band of Indians would try to steal horses or a cow or two from them.

When it was getting late, Sam excused himself and went out to the barn. He needed time to think. Bessie and Billy had been on his mind a lot over the past few days. Sam had grown to like Billy, and his mother seemed like a very special woman. They seemed to understand what was required of them to make a home on the prairie, and what it took to defend it.

Sam had been thinking about settling down. He had thought about giving up being a lawman several times over the past couple of years, but it was the first time he had felt so strongly about it. The idea of settling down there had crossed his mind several times, too.

Sam was leaning against one of the stalls and thinking about what was going to happen to Bessie and Billy if he left, when he glanced at the saddles and saddlebags that had belonged to the Morgan brothers. The one thing he had not done was go through the saddlebags.

He gathered the saddlebags and hung them over a stall railing, then began looking at what was in them. Most of what was there would be of little use to Bessie and Billy, but there were several things they could use.

Sam found several small pouches of gold coins that had been stolen in one of the many robberies the Morgan brothers had done. It would have to be returned. There was ammunition for the guns which were now in the possession of Bessie and Billy. He also found small amounts of sugar, flour and coffee, and a few metal cups and plates. Of course, there were the three horses and saddles that could be used or sold.

Sam knew there were rewards for all of the Morgan brothers. It was only right that it be given to Bessie. That would surely give Bessie and Billy enough money to help them buy a few head of cattle if they changed their minds and decided to stay. He couldn't help but think that their little farm would be better suited for the country as a cattle ranch.

Sam came up with an idea. He would put the saddlebags under the Christmas tree for them to find on Christmas morning. He would write a note about the reward money and put it under the tree, too. Sam spent the next hour taking everything out of the saddlebags that was of no use to Bessie and Billy, but left anything they could use.

Sam had just finished when he heard someone behind him. He turned and saw Bessie come in the barn. He smiled at her.

"I thought I would come out and see what is taking you so long," she said as she walked up to him. "It is getting late."

"I was just thinking."

"What about, if I might ask?"

"About you and Billy."

Sam looked down at the ground and pushed a little of the dirt around with his foot. He was feeling a bit embarrassed. His life had been a lonely one, and he was thinking it was time for a change. He had been thinking about staying and making a home for the three of them. The problem was, he didn't know what Bessie would think of the idea, and he didn't know how to tell her.

"I saved your life," Bessie reminded him. "I think that you could at least tell me what you were thinking since it was about Billy and me."

Sam looked up at her. She was right. He owed her that much.

"You might be right, but you might not like what I was thinking."

"Oh," she said as she looked up at him. "Why don't you let me decide. I might like it."

"Okay. I was thinking it was time for me to give up being a lawman and become a rancher."

"Oh. And where were you thinking about doing that?" she asked with smile.

He wasn't sure, but he got the feeling that she knew what he had been thinking. If that was the case, anything he said would not be much of a surprise.

"I was thinking of sticking around here and seeing how things might work out, you know, between us."

"And just how would you like things to work out?"

"I would like to turn this farm into a ranch. We could get some cattle and raise them here. There is plenty of land, and the grass is good. I even know where we could get some good breeding stock for the ranch. We have several horses now."

He suddenly stopped talking as he looked at her. She was smiling at him.

"You said 'we.' Does that mean you want to stay here with Billy and me?"

Bessie had a big smile on her face and a sparkle in her eyes.

"Yes," he admitted softly, almost embarrassed to say it.

"I would like that. I would like that very much," she said as she stepped closer to him.

"I would like that very much, too."

"Then we need to start making plans, don't you think?"

"Yes. I guess we do."

"But not out here in the barn. It's too cold out here for that. Come inside."

"Are you sure?"

"Yes. Billy would like you to stay here with us, too."

"What will people say if we are living together and not married?" he asked.

"We rarely have visitors, and those that come by wouldn't know if we are married or not."

"Maybe some day we could find us a preacher and get married?"

"Yes, that would be nice. Now, it's getting late. We need to get some sleep. We have a lot of plans to make, starting tomorrow."

"Yes, ma'am," he said with a smile.

"Don't call me, ma'am. Call me, Bessie, please," she said as she took hold of his hand and led him to the cabin."

Bessie and Sam made the place into a ranch. During the following summer a preacher came by and they were married. The ranch grew over the years and became a large cattle ranch. They had several children. The years were good to them and they grew old together on their ranch.

MAIL-ORDER BRIDE

The sound of the locomotive's whistle announced the arrival of a train to the town of Spearfish in the Dakota Territory. A young woman sat staring out the coach window as the train rolled to a stop in front of the station. She knew that it was where she was to leave the train, but she hesitated. The woman watched as the other passengers got off the train. She could see them smile as they were greeted by people they knew.

Finally, the woman got up and moved to the end of the coach, then stepped off onto the station platform. The woman took only a few steps away from the train before she stopped and began to look for the man who was to meet her, but he was nowhere in sight. The expression on the young woman's face gave the impression that she might be lost, and a little scared.

The woman was fairly tall and carried herself well. As she stood on the platform, she set her carpetbag and brown paper sack down next to her feet. She brushed the skirt of her simple cotton dress, then straightened the white hand knitted shawl over her shoulders. Although she was a beautiful young woman, she didn't appear to have come from a family of wealth. In fact, she looked to be rather poor.

The sound of the train's whistle caused her to abruptly turn around. She took a step toward the train, but stopped. She thought about getting back on the train before she was left all alone in a strange town, but she couldn't.

Once the train was gone, she turned and looked up and down the station platform. Still no one had come to meet her. Not knowing what else to do, she picked up her carpetbag and sack, then walked to a bench and sat down to wait. All the passengers had gone, leaving her feeling abandoned.

The man she had expected to meet had not shown up, which caused her to wonder if he had changed his mind about marrying her. Maybe something had happened to him. Maybe he was sick or injured somewhere.

Maybe he didn't get her letter telling him when she would arrive. All sorts of thoughts passed through her mind as to why he wasn't there.

While she waited, she began to wonder if coming all the way out west had been a good idea. She could hardly believe she had agreed to come so far from everything she knew to marry a man that she had never met. She had a picture of him so she knew what he looked like. He had written her long letters telling her about his ranch, his plans and his dreams for the future, but she had never actually talked to him. He had sent her the money she would need to make the trip.

The longer she waited, the more she thought it had been a mistake. She felt as if she didn't belong there, but then she didn't really know where she belonged. It crossed her mind that maybe it would be best if she took the first train back, but she knew she could not do that. She didn't have the money for a return trip ticket, and there was nothing for her back east. She was beginning to feel trapped.

The young woman thought about what she would do if no one came to get her. She had a little money, but not enough to get a room at the hotel and something to eat.

Suddenly, her thoughts were disturbed by the sound of someone walking toward her. She glanced up hoping it was the man she had come to marry, but it was an older gentleman wearing a black suit and black hat. The man walked up to her, removed his hat and looked down at her.

"Good afternoon," the elderly gentleman said with a pleasant smile. "I'm Reverend Frank Wilcox. Are you Miss Anna Gardner?"

"Yes," she replied shyly as she looked into the man's tired eyes.

"I'm pleased to finally meet you. Mr. Jenkins has told me so much about you."

"I thought Henry would be here to meet me,"

"He has been detained, but he will be here tomorrow. He asked me to meet you."

"Oh," she said wondering what she was going to do and where was she going to stay.

The fact she would have to wait to meet Henry disappointed her. She had spent the entire trip thinking about him and hoping that all would be well between them when they finally met.

"I'm sorry, but we best be going. I have a buggy in front of the station."

"Where are we going?" she asked, not sure she wanted to go with him.

"You will be spending the night with my wife and me. Tomorrow, Henry will arrive and you will be married in the church. You will then go to his ranch as his wife."

"Thank you," she said, as she looked at him.

Anna was not sure she should be thanking him. It seemed that everything was going wrong, at least not as she had anticipated. She remembered reading in one of Henry's letters that he couldn't wait to show her his ranch.

"Do you have anything else?"

The Reverend had disturbed her thoughts. Anna looked at him before she replied.

"No," she said softly. "This is all I have."

"Let me help you," he said as he reached down and picked up her carpetbag. "Mrs. Wilcox is waiting to meet you."

Reverend Wilcox started toward the front of the station. Anna followed along behind as if she didn't want to go with him, but she really had no choice. If she didn't go with him, she would have no place to spend the night.

Anna got into the buggy. The Reverend drove the buggy down the street while Anna looked around. It was not much of a town compared to Chicago. There was a general store, a blacksmith's shop and livery stable. She also noticed there was a hotel, a couple of saloons, a bank and a few smaller stores like a bakery, a café and a leather shop.

It didn't take them long to get to the Reverend's house. It was a two story white house with a large front porch. There was a white clapboard church next to the house.

When the buggy came to a stop in front of the house, Anna looked up at it. She wondered what Henry's house might look like.

"Anna," the Reverend said to get her attention.

Anna looked at the Reverend, then got out of the buggy. She followed him into the house. Once inside, she saw a short older woman come out of the kitchen. The woman was wiping her hands on her flowered apron. She was a pleasant looking woman with short brown hair.

"Emma, this is Anna Gardner," the Reverend said.

"Come in my dear. Please make yourself at home. Dinner will be ready shortly. Frank, please take her things up to the guest room."

Anna handed her sack to the Reverend, then watched him as he took her things up the stairs to the second floor. She had a strange feeling come over her as he walked away with everything that she owned in the world, but her attention quickly shifted to Emma.

"If you would like to wash up a little before dinner, you can come out in the kitchen. The outhouse is out the backdoor and to the left if you have need of it," Emma said.

Anna followed Emma to the kitchen. She washed up, then turned to watch Emma as she took a large Dutch oven out of the wood burning stove. When she took the top off, there was a large pot roast inside. It smelled wonderful. Anna could not remember ever seeing such a large roast. In with the roast were potatoes, carrots and onions. To Anna it was a meal fit for a king. She had been lucky to get soup with very little meat and a few vegetables in it, and bread at the orphanage where she grew up.

"Can I help you with anything?" Anna asked as she watched Emma scoop the potatoes from the roasting pan and placed them in a bowl.

"Thank you. If you would like, you can take the potatoes into the dining room."

Anna took the bowl of potatoes into the dining room and set it on the table. The table was set with beautiful dishes trimmed in a flowery blue pattern, and sparkling silverware. There were silver candle holders as well. The table was covered with a large delicate lace tablecloth, too.

Anna had never seen a table set like this one. It looked like something out of one of the magazines she had seen in Chicago. All the silverware at the orphanage had been mismatched; most of the dishes were old and chipped, and there was never a tablecloth.

Everything was so perfect that it caused her to wonder if Henry might have such beautiful things in his house. Being that he was a rancher and a bachelor, he probably didn't have any fancy dishes or silverware, she thought.

Emma brought in a platter with the pot roast surrounded by carrots and onions. The Reverend followed his wife into the dining room with a pitcher of milk, something that was only seen at breakfast in the orphanage, and then they were only allowed a small cup of it to put on their oatmeal.

Emma could see the look on Anna's face as Anna looked at the table. Emma had some idea of what might be running through Anna's mind, but decided not to say anything.

"Please, Anna, sit down," Emma said as she pointed to a chair.

As soon as they were seated, the Reverend said a short prayer then began passing the food around. He noticed Anna seemed to be very careful with everything. He also noticed that she took fairly small portions. He was sure that it was the result of being raised in an orphanage where there was probably little food to go around.

"Anna, please tell us a little about yourself. All we know about you is what Henry has told us from your letters," Emma said.

Anna looked at Emma and then at the Reverend. These people were strangers to her, but they had taken her into their home. They were providing her with a place to sleep and food to eat. It seemed unfair not to tell them about herself.

"As you know, I'm what they call a mail-order bride. I lost my parents when I was very young. Since I had no family to take me in, I grew up in an orphanage in Chicago. I had to leave the orphanage because I'm too old to stay there.

"One of the other girls who had lived at the orphanage told me about a couple who was arranging marriages to men who lived out west. They said that there weren't very many women in the west."

"That certainly is true enough," the Reverend said.

"Well, my friend told me that she had met a very nice man on one of his trips to Chicago. When he returned to his ranch, he began writing to her. She wrote back to him. They became close through their letters, and he wrote asking her to marry him. She wrote back that she would, and he sent her the money to go west to marry him. I didn't know what else to do, so I talked to the same couple who had helped my friend."

"Did you get to meet Henry before you came out here?"

"No, but he sent me a picture of himself. I have never met him, but he sounded very nice in his letters. He told me all about his ranch."

"How long have you been writing to each other?" Emma asked.

"It has been almost eight months."

The Reverend looked at his wife and she looked at him. Anna wondered what was going on between them. It didn't seem that they looked very happy at the moment. She wondered if they were keeping something from her.

"Excuse me, but is there something wrong, or something that I should know?" Anna asked.

"No," the Reverend said. "It doesn't seem very long to get to know each other, especially by mail."

Anna looked at him. She guessed that it might not be very long to him, but it seemed like a long time to her.

"Go on, please," Emma said, encouraging her to tell them more about herself.

"Anyway, we started writing back and forth in order to get acquainted. Then in one of his letters he asked me to marry him. I wrote back and told him that I would, and he sent me the money to buy a ticket for the train to Spearfish.

"I was supposed to meet Henry here. If our meeting goes well and we seem to get along, then I am to marry him and move to his ranch.

It was my understanding that I was to stay in town while we get to know each other."

"Well, I think there might have been a little misunderstanding," the Reverend said. "It was our understanding that you would meet him here. You are to be married, and then the two of you go to his ranch as husband and wife. There was nothing said about spending time to get to know each other before the wedding. It was thought that your letters took care of that."

"Oh, my. I thought I would have a chance to talk to him for a little while before I had to marry him and live on his ranch."

"How much time do you think you will need?" Emma asked.

"I thought that I would have a day or two to get to know him on a more personal level before we married," she said as a twinge of panic began to grip her.

"It is all arranged. Henry doesn't like to be away from his ranch very long. He is a very busy man," the Reverend said.

"I understand that, but why would he want to marry someone he has never even seen without at least having a little time for us to talk to each other?"

"He is expecting you to marry him tomorrow. He has work to do on the ranch, especially this time of year. He is expecting you to do your share," Emma said as she looked at Anna.

Anna just looked at Emma. What did she mean by "do your share"? She was expected to do her share of the work as his wife. But the way it sounded when Emma said it, made it sound as if it was more like Henry was marrying her to have someone to work for him. Not someone to be his wife and partner in the ranching.

All she could think about was what she had gotten herself into. There was nothing she could do about it tonight. She would talk to Henry tomorrow and try to work things out with him before the wedding. Maybe it would not be so bad, but she had to at least talk to him before she married him.

Nothing more was said about tomorrow at the table. Anna helped Emma take the dishes and leftover food to the kitchen when everyone was finished. Emma washed while Anna dried the dishes and carefully stacked them on the table. She didn't talk much. She was busy thinking about tomorrow. Her thoughts of what might happen to her if things didn't work out ran through her head. Although, she had started out with high hopes, there were doubts that continued to creep into her thoughts. There had been nothing to relieve her doubts, so far.

"I think we are done here," Emma said with a smile. "I'm sure you would like to get some rest. It has been a long day for you."

"Yes, it has," Anna replied.

"Your room is the second door on the left at the top of the stairs. I hope you rest well."

"Thank you."

Anna hung up the towel and said goodnight. She then immediately went upstairs to her room and got ready for bed.

Anna's mind filled with worries and fears about what tomorrow might bring. All she knew about Henry was what he had told her in his letters. She couldn't marry him without finding out something about him. The thought crossed her mind that maybe she should leave before it was too late, but where would she go? There was nowhere she could go without money.

As she laid in the bed looking up at the ceiling, she came up with a plan. She would get up and have breakfast, then take a walk around town. She would talk to some of the shopkeepers. Maybe she could get an idea of what kind of a man Henry really was. With that thought planted firmly in her mind, she was able to fall asleep.

* * * *

When morning came, Anna was up and dressed and ready for breakfast. When she walked into the kitchen, she found the Reverend sitting at the table. Emma was serving him.

"Good morning. You may sit over there," Emma said as she pointed to a chair next to the Reverend.

"Reverend, what time do you think Henry should arrive in town?"

"I would think that it wouldn't be very much before noon," he replied.

"I was thinking that I would like to take a walk around town. I have a few things I would like to get at the General Store. I didn't bring very much with me, and I have a little money left."

"I could go with you and help you pick out the things you might need," Emma said.

"I'm sorry, Emma, but I was also going to use the time to think about some of the things I would like to ask Henry when he gets here."

"I think it would be all right, Emma," the Reverend said. "After all, marriage is an important decision."

Anna wondered what the Reverend's comment meant. Why would it not be all right? First of all, she was not married to Henry, yet, and secondly, she was not a prisoner. The word "prisoner" struck her as a strange word to have come to mind. Was she beginning to think that she might end up a prisoner if she married Henry?

"Yes, it is," Emma agreed. "Maybe after you get settled in your new life, we could go shopping together."

"Yes, that would be nice," Anna said.

As she ate her breakfast, she realized that she was not a prisoner, but she was indebted to Henry. He had paid for her trip to Spearfish based on his belief that she would marry him. If she failed to marry him, she would owe him the money he had sent her. Maybe it would be all right, but she still wanted to talk to someone who might know him.

When breakfast was over, Anna put on her bonnet and headed for the General Store. It was not a very big store, but it had a good variety of merchandise. She took a few minutes to look around the store before she went up to the counter. The man at the counter looked up at her and smiled.

"Can I help you with something?" the storekeeper asked.

"Yes. I know that you don't know me, but I would like to know if you have any contact with Mr. Henry Jenkins?"

"Sure. He does a lot of business in my store."

"I was wondering if you could tell me something about him. What kind of a man is he?"

"Excuse me, but why do you want to know that?" the storekeeper asked.

"Well, it is kind of hard to explain."

"You're Anna Gardner. Am I correct?" the woman standing off to the side asked.

Anna turned and looked at the woman. The woman appeared to be few years younger than the storekeeper. She was wearing a blue cotton dress with a plain white apron over it. Her hair was pulled back in a bun, and she had a pencil stuck in it.

"Yes, I am," she replied, somewhat surprised that the woman would know of her.

"Hans, this is the woman who has come from back east to marry Henry," she said with a note of excitement in her voice.

"Well, now. Henry said you were pretty, but he didn't say how pretty."

"Thank you," Anna said.

"I'm Greta Swenson and this is Hans, my husband. It is so good to meet you."

"Thank you," Anna said, not sure what else to say.

"Oh, forgive me. I think I understand why you came in. Do you have time for a cup of tea?" Greta asked as she smiled at Anna.

"Yes."

"Hans, Anna and I are going to have a visit. I'll be back in a little while."

"I can see this will be women's talk. You two have a nice talk. I'll finish the order."

Greta took Anna by the arm and gently led her to the back of the store where the Swensons lived. Greta pointed to a chair at a table where Anna could sit down, then immediately put a kettle of water on the stove to heat.

"I think I can understand how you must feel about now."

Anna looked at the woman wondering if she really did understand.

"I was not a mail-order bride, but I married Hans without knowing him very well. You are here to try to find out if the man who asked you to marry him is a good man. Am I right?"

"Well, yes," Anna answered shyly.

"Henry is a good man. Now, that's not to say he's perfect, but what man is. Henry is a little rough around the edges, if you know what I mean."

"I'm not sure I understand," Anna said, looking a little puzzled.

"He has lived a long time with no one around to talk to but other men and cattle."

"Is he a violent man?" she asked, a little worried about the answer.

"Oh, heavens no. He can be violent when it is necessary, like most western men. You have to remember that this is still a wild and hard country out here. There are often times when the only law is the law that a man can back up himself. Sometimes it is necessary to enforce the law yourself in order to get justice. Someday it will not be that way, but until that day a man has to enforce the laws himself."

"I think I understand that. I'm a little worried about how he will treat me."

"Henry is a rare sort of man," Greta said with a grin. "He is the type of man who would do anything for the woman he cares about, and I can assure you that Henry cares very much for you.

"Does he drink?"

"Like most ranchers and cowboys, he sometimes drinks a little too much, but he is not a drunkard. He will have a drink with the men from time to time, but I have never seen him fallen-down-drunk."

"What is his ranch like? Have you seen it?"

"Yes, I have. It is nothing fancy, but I don't think you can expect anything more from a man. But with a woman's touch, it could be a very nice place to live."

Anna sat and looked at Greta. She wondered if what she was told was true. She could not think of one reason for Greta to lie to her.

"Anna, if you could have seen his face whenever he got a letter from you, you would have no doubt that he is already in love with you. When he got your picture, he showed it to everyone. I've never seen a man so happy."

Anna smiled at her comment. She remembered her surprise at getting his picture. She thought he was handsome.

Greta poured a cup of tea for each of them, then sat down at the table. Greta told her everything she knew about Henry. They spent a good hour drinking tea and talking about him. When it was getting time for Anna to return to the Reverend's house, she thanked Greta for spending the time with her.

"Anna, you have to give Henry a chance to get to know you. He will make a good husband, but it will take time for the two of you to get to know and understand each other. I hope that you give him the chance. And remember, he needs you as much as you need him. You have to work together."

"Thank you for the advice. I will remember it," Anna said as she stood up to leave.

"When is the wedding?"

"I'm not sure, but I was told he would be coming into town before noon and that we will be married this afternoon."

"If you can, let me know. I will come."

"I would like that," Anna said with a smile.

Anna left the General Store and walked back toward the Reverend's house. On the walk back to the house, Anna was thinking that she might have found a friend in Greta. She also felt a little more comfortable about marrying Henry.

When she arrived at the house, she noticed a buggy out in front. She had a feeling that it belonged to Henry. Entering the house, she saw a man sitting on a chair in the parlor. She immediately recognized the man as Henry. He was wearing a suit that didn't fit him very well, and he looked a little uncomfortable in it. She was sure that he was more comfortable in his work clothes. She watched him as he stood up, turned toward her and smiled. He was taller than she had expected.

"Hi," was all Henry could manage to say.

"Hi," Anna replied shyly.

"I'm Henry," he said as he looked her over. "You are about the prettiest thing I think I've ever seen."

Anna blushed at his comment and looked down at the floor.

"I'm sorry, Ma'am, I didn't mean to embarrass you," he said as he took a step toward her, then stopped.

Anna looked up at him. She quickly realized that he was as nervous about meeting her as she was about meeting him.

"It's okay, Henry," she said shyly.

"Anna, do you still need some time before the wedding to talk to Henry?" Emma said.

Anna turned and looked at Emma. She realized that her talk with Greta had done a lot to make her feel more comfortable about marrying Henry.

"I don't think that will be necessary. There is one thing. I would like to invite Greta Swenson and her husband to our wedding. That is if you don't mind, Henry."

"I don't mind. They're good people. You want me to go ask them to come?"

"Henry, since you are already dressed in your Sunday best, why don't you go ask them while we get things ready here," Reverend

Wilcox said. "Have them come to the church."

"Sure thing, Reverend."

Henry looked at Anna and smiled, then turned and left the Reverend's house.

"Do you have a wedding dress?" Emma asked as soon as Henry had left.

"No," she replied softly, looking a little embarrassed.

"That's okay," Emma said. "I have my sister's wedding dress upstairs. I think we can make it work, if you would like."

"That would be nice."

Emma and Anna went upstairs to see if the wedding dress would fit. In the meantime, Reverend Wilcox went to the church to get things ready there.

Emma and Anna arrived at the church just a few minutes after the Swensons. Anna looked at Henry as he stood next to Reverend Wilcox at the front of the church. She thought he looked handsome in his suit, even if it didn't fit him all that well.

Anna was wearing a borrowed wedding dress. The dress was white and a little big for her, but with a little extra pinning here and there, it fit her well. Emma also gave Anna a small bouquet of pink and red roses from her flower bed alongside the house.

Emma sat down at the pedal organ and began to play. Anna wasn't sure what she was playing, but it didn't matter. She was now ready to marry Henry. Anna was still a little nervous as she walked down the aisle with the bouquet of flowers in her hands. The closer she got to Henry, the better she was feeling about marrying him.

After all the words had been said and the Reverend had pronounced them man and wife, Henry leaned down to kiss his new bride.

Anna closed her eyes and waited for his lips to meet hers. She was a little surprised that his kiss was so light and tender. After he kissed her, she looked up at him and smiled. There was something about this man, a man she didn't even know, that made her want to make their marriage work.

"Dinner is ready at the house for all present," Emma announced. "I know it is a long trip back to the ranch for Henry and

Anna, but a good meal before they start back will be good."

Henry looked down at Anna, then took her hand. They started out of the church.

"I hope you like my place, - ah - I mean our place," Henry said as he looked at her for some kind of reaction.

"I'm sure I will."

"We can fix it up any way you like. Maybe Greta could help you pick out some cloth for curtains."

"I'd like that," Anna said as she looked up at him.

They went into the Reverend's house with everyone else. Once they were all seated around the dining room table, the Reverend said a short prayer before they started to eat.

Anna found herself glancing over at her new husband during the dinner. When he would glance at her, she would smile at him and look a little embarrassed.

When dinner was finished, the Swensons gave the newlyweds a gift. Anna and Henry opened it to find several large pieces of cloth, some notions, and a couple of jars of homemade jam.

"The cloth is for window curtains, or to make dresses," Greta said.

"I'm sure Henry doesn't have any curtains," Hans said with a laugh.

"I can assure you that Henry doesn't have curtains." the Reverend said jokingly.

Anna smiled when she looked at Henry and saw that he was embarrassed. But she was pleased that he took the ribbing with a sense of humor.

"You never know. I might just have a couple of dresses in the closet for my new bride," he said, then looked at Anna and grinned.

"We have a little something for the newlyweds, too," Emma said, then stood up and got a box from the floor. Emma set the box on a chair next to Anna and said, "This is for you and your new home."

"Thank you. It is so kind of all of you."

"Are you going to open it?" Hans asked.

Anna opened the box and discovered a four place setting of dishes. The dishes were beautiful. They had a ring of delicate red flowers around the edges of the plates and a red edge on all the pieces.

"There're lovely," Anna said as her breath caught.

Anna had only seen such beautiful dishes one time before, and that was at Emma's table. She was choked up that someone would give her such beautiful dishes.

"You shouldn't have," she said as a tear rolled down her cheek and she looked at Emma.

"If she hadn't, you would be eating off metal pie pans," the Reverend said with a laugh.

"That's not so," Henry said, then turned to Anna. "I had Hans send off for a four place setting of dishes just so you could eat off real dishes. I got some glasses and matching dinnerware, too."

"You might want to look at the dishes," Hans said to Henry with a grin. "The ones you had me order are the same pattern. Now you have enough dishes to have all of us to dinner."

"I guess we will have to have them all come out to the ranch for dinner sometime," Anna said as she looked at Henry.

"I guess so," Henry said as he looked at his new bride and grinned.

"As much as I would like this little party to continue, the newlyweds had better get on the road home, or they won't get there before dark," the Reverend said.

With that said, all of them got up and followed the newlyweds outside. Henry helped his new bride up onto the seat while Hans and the Reverend put their gifts in the buggy. Henry climbed up beside Anna. They turned and looked at their friends.

"Thank you all for making this a wonderful day," Anna said.

"It was our pleasure," the Reverend said. "Now get along."

Henry turned the horse toward the road home then started out. As they left town, he looked at Anna and smiled. She smiled back at him as she slipped her arm in his.

Anna no longer had any misgivings about her marriage to Henry. She was sure anything that came up, they could deal with together. For the first time in her life, Anna felt like she was where she belonged, and with the man she was destined to be with for the rest of her life.

THE GOLDEN EAGLE MINE

On a warm day in the early spring of 1886, an old man was chipping away at some loose rocks deep in the Black Hills of the Dakota Territory. As he hit the rock with his pick, one more time for luck, a piece of rock fell away exposing a long narrow vein of gold. His eyes got big at the sight of gold that ran back in along a fissure. He looked up at the sky as if to give thanks when he noticed a large Golden Eagle sitting on a branch looking down at him. He smiled at the eagle, then turned back and began swinging his pick at the rock. He gathered up the small pieces of gold as they fell at his feet. He had several ounces of the yellow mineral after only a few hours.

After working several hours, he was beginning to feel hungry. He put down his pick and picked up his rifle. He then went off to find his dinner. It wasn't long before he returned with a rabbit. While skinning and preparing the rabbit to cook, he noticed that the eagle had returned. He smiled, then cut off a piece of the raw meat and tossed it on the ground below the eagle.

The eagle looked from the meat to the old man for several minutes before it flew off the branch and landed on the ground near the meat. The bird grabbed the meat in its beak, then flew back up into the tree. With one eye on the old man, it began to eat the piece of meat. The bird stayed around until just before dark when it flew away.

Over the next few months, the old man worked in his mine. Each evening the eagle would return and sit on the branch while the old man prepared his dinner. And each night the old man would share what he had to eat with the eagle.

As time passed, it became clear that it would take a long time for the old man to get all of the gold the rock had to offer. He decided he needed a place where he could get out of the weather, so he built a small cabin with a fireplace. It was just big enough to have a place to lay down to rest, a place to fix his meals and a place to get in out of the rain and cold.

Once he had his cabin finished, he began working in his mine again. He spent the better part of the winter working in the mine. He only took time off to hunt for food, to get water and to gather wood for his fireplace.

By spring, the old man had grown tired. Working every day in the mine had taken a toll on him. He decided that it was time to slow down and relax a little each day. After all, he had taken out more gold than he had ever seen before. He began by putting in a small vegetable garden next to the cabin.

As he was taking a break on a late summer morning, the old man began to think about his mine. He was sure that he had found the place where he wanted to spend the rest of his life, and where he could do what he knew how to do best, be a miner.

He also began to think about what he should call his mine. He knew that some of the big mines in California and Nevada had names. Why shouldn't his mine have a name? After all, it was producing a fair amount of gold. The mine may not be as big as other mines, but it was deserving of a name just the same. The name he wanted for his mine had to be something special.

As he sat drinking coffee one morning, the large Golden Eagle landed on the branch of a large tree that hung over the mine entrance. He looked at the eagle as it looked back at him. A smile slowly came over the old man's face.

"Okay, big fella, we'll call it The Golden Eagle Mine."

The eagle looked at him and tipped its head to one side. It sort of bobbed its head as if to agree, then flew away. He watched the eagle as it disappeared over a distant ridge.

The old man continued to work in the mine every day, and every day the eagle would land in the tree and watch him as he took his midmorning coffee break. He even took time out to carve the name of the mine in the rock over the entrance. In the evening, the bird would show up for dinner.

One day while the old man was sitting in front of his cabin enjoying his usual midmorning cup of coffee, two men rode up. He didn't like the looks of them one bit.

"Can I do somethin' for you fellas?" he asked as he looked the two men over.

"We hear that you've been doin' pretty good up here. We was thinkin' 'bout doin' a little minin' ourselves," one of the men said as he smiled down from his horse.

"Well, I laid claim to this here area. If you're goin' to mine around here, you'll need to move out a little ways that way," he said as he pointed toward the west.

The two men looked in the direction that the old man pointed, then turned and looked back at him.

"How far we got ta go ta be off your claim?" the other man asked.

"Oh, about a mile, maybe a mite more. Just past them rocks that look like large poles," he said as he pointed at the rocks on the other side of the valley.

"Thanks, Mister. We'll go that way."

The old man nodded and watched them as they rode toward the west. He was nobody's fool. He knew right off that those two were not miners. Neither of them looked like they had worked a day in their lives. The muscles in their arms were not hard like someone who worked hard. Even if they were planning to become miners, they didn't have the tools to do any mining. The only thing he was sure of was that they were up to no good.

That evening as he was fixing his dinner in his cabin, he heard a horse whinny. He had a feeling that it was the two men who had come by earlier in the day. The old man quickly picked up his rifle, then blew out the lamp on the table. He moved to a window and carefully looked out.

At first he didn't see anything. It was dark except for some moonlight that helped make it possible to see something, but only if it moved. It wasn't until he noticed some movement behind a bush that he got an idea of where they were hiding. There was just a shadowy figure behind the bush, but it was enough for him to know it was a man. He aimed his rifle toward the bush and fired a shot. He had aimed the shot high as a warning. It was a warning to let them know that he would defend what he had worked hard to build.

"You're goin' ta have ta shoot better than that, old man," one of the men called out with a chuckle in his voice.

The old man recognized the voice of the man. It was one of the two men he had seen earlier that day. He fired another shot, only he fired it into the bush where he had seen movement.

"You ain't gettin' my mine, and you'll pay a heavy price tryin'," the old man yelled out at them.

"We got ourselves a couple sticks of dynamite. We're goin' ta get ya out of that cabin if we have ta blow it up."

Just then he saw a match flare up. He took a quick shot toward the light and heard someone scream in pain. He quickly crawled under his bed and slipped out the trap door he had made in the wall at the back of the cabin. He then crawled off into the woods. He had just slipped into the woods when a stick of dynamite went through the window. The dynamite exploded completely destroying the cabin.

The old man watched from his hiding place behind some bushes as the two men walked up to the cabin and looked at what was left of it. They began to grin.

"That should take care of him. I think we got us a mine, George."

"I think you're right, Wilber."

"Now what do we do?"

"We set up camp over there by them trees and get this wound taken care of," George said as he looked at the scratch on his arm.

"It hurt much?"

"Nah. It's just a scratch. It done scared me more than hurt. I didn't think he could hit me."

Wilber built a fire, then cleaned and dressed the scratch on George's arm. When he was finished, they set up camp next to the fire.

"Let's get us a good night's sleep. Tomorrow we start checkin' out the mine," George said.

"Ya think he found anythin' in there?"

"He's been workin' this mine for a long time. I'd be willin' ta bet he's found plenty of gold. If we don't find nothin' in the mine, we'll sort through what's left of the cabin. He might have been keeping it there."

"I think that's a good idea, George."

It was late and the moon wasn't as bright as it had been earlier. The old man saw that they had laid out their bedrolls near the fire. He waited. When he was sure they were both sound asleep, he took a bullet from his rifle and tossed it into the red hot coals of the fire.

George and Wilber hadn't been asleep very long when their sleep was rudely interrupted by a sudden loud bang. The two men sat straight up and grabbed for their guns. They looked around, but didn't see anyone. All they saw was a large ball of smoke and ash rising from the hot coals of the fire.

"What the heck was that?" Wilber asked as he looked at George.

Wilber was very nervous. His eyes were big as he looked first one way than the other, but saw nothing.

"It looks like ya built the fire on top of a cartridge someone dropped. The heat must of caused the darn thin' ta explode."

"Ya think there might be another one?"

"I doubt it. The fire's almost out. We should try ta get us some sleep."

"Okay, but I don't like it," Wilber said as he lay back down.

Wilber couldn't go back to sleep right away, his nerves were on edge. The sound of the shot going off in the fire had scared him. After a while he noticed George was snoring and that the fire had gone completely out. It was only then that he was able to close his eyes, but sleep still didn't come easy.

When morning came, Wilber was up with the sun. He had not slept well. Every little sound in the night from the ruffling of a leaf in the breeze to the sound of an owl taking flight woke him.

As Wilber sat on his bedroll and looked around, he saw an eagle land on a branch above the mine entrance. The eagle sat there and stared back at him. He felt a cold shiver go down his spine. For some reason, the eagle frightened him. He was afraid to move for fear the eagle would attack him.

Suddenly, the eagle took flight. It dove toward Wilber and flew right over his head, missing him by inches. Wilber screamed as he ducked down and covered his head. He was sure that the eagle was attacking him, but it simply flew off to land on a tree branch near the remains of the old man's cabin. The eagle sat there for a moment looking from the rubble of the cabin to Wilber before it flew to another tree.

"What the heck's all the racket," George said as he sat up and looked at Wilber.

"That eagle attacked me," Wilber said, his voice showing how scared he was as he pointed toward the eagle.

"Don't be a fool. An eagle won't attack a man."

"Well, that one did. He's darn right mad 'bout somethin'. Ya think he's a friend of that old man?"

"Oh, for crying out loud. Forget the darn eagle and get breakfast started. We've got a gold mine ta check out."

Wilber looked at George. He was angry that George didn't believe him and he was getting bossy. But on the other hand, he was right. They did have a gold mine to check out, and his hopes were high that they might find the old man's gold.

Wilber got up and shook out his boots. He didn't want some little critter crawling around inside his boots while he was trying to put them on. He also continued to watch the eagle. After a short time the eagle flew away, much to Wilber's relief.

Wilber gathered some wood for a fire and got it started. He built the fire in the same place he had built the fire the previous night. He figured there wouldn't be any more cartridges there that would explode.

All the time Wilber was fixing breakfast, he kept an eye on the sky. He didn't want the eagle to come back to attack him again. The eagle had really rattled his nerves.

When they were finished eating, Wilber cleaned up while George was looking over the entrance to the mine. When he was finished cleaning up, he walked over to the mine.

"We goin' in the mine?" Wilber asked as he wondered why George didn't enter the mine.

"Yeah. You go first."

Wilber looked at George. He wondered why George would want him to go first. They had been friends for years, but all of a sudden Wilber wasn't sure he trusted George anymore. Maybe George thought there was a trap inside the mine.

In spite of his feelings, he cautiously moved past George and went into the mine. On a shelf just inside the entrance was a box of matches and a coal oil lamp. Wilber lit the lamp and turned to look down the tunnel.

"See anythin'?" George asked still standing outside the mine.

"Just rock."

"Maybe we should go deeper inta the mine," George suggested.

Wilber started slowly moving deeper into the mine. He was feeling a little uncomfortable with George following behind him. Then it came to him. It was at that moment he remembered George was afraid of enclosed spaces, especially dark spaces, yet he was in the mine. It was apparent that George's thirst for gold was stronger than his fear of closed dark places.

They had worked their way deep into the mine when they heard a loud noise that seemed to fill the tunnel. With the noise echoing around and around inside the tunnel, it was impossible to tell where it had come from, or what had made the noise.

"What was that?" Wilber asked, his voice showing the noise had frightened him.

"I don't know," George said as he looked into the darkness of the tunnel.

"Do ya think there was a cave-in?"

"I don't know, but it sounded more like the wind."

The two men stood there first looking one way then the other. Whatever the noise was, it had made them very nervous and a bit jumpy.

"I think we should get outa here," Wilber said, his voice showing how terrified he was of the weird noise.

"Not so fast. Let's wait and see if we hear it again."

They stood there in silence. The light from the coal lamp was not giving off a great deal of light. They could see nothing beyond a few yards. The only thing they could hear was the sound of their own breathing. It seemed like they stood there forever, listening.

Suddenly, they heard the sound again. Only this time there seemed to be a voice in the wind. It was as if the wind was talking to them, but they couldn't understand what it was saying. Wilber turned and was about to run, but George grabbed his arm.

"Ya heard that, didn't ya?" Wilber asked, his voice trembling with fear.

"It was just the wind. There must be some place where the wind gets in here."

"No. It was a voice warnin' us ta get outa here while we still can," Wilber said, his voice quivering as he spoke.

"We're not leavin' 'til we find the gold," George said sharply.

Just then they heard what sounded like a voice. It came as almost a whisper, but it sounded a little like the old man.

"You shouldn't have killed me," the whispery voice said.

"Ya hear that?" Wilber said as his heart began to race.

"Yeah. I heard it. It seems that we didn't kill the old man."

"That was the old man's ghost," Wilber insisted.

"Get hold of yourself. There ain't no such thin' as ghosts."

"I want outa here," Wilber screamed.

He jerked his arm free of George's grip and started to run for the entrance of the cave with the lamp in his hand. Within seconds he had left George standing alone in the dark mine.

"Get back here," George yelled as the light from the lamp disappeared.

Wilber paid no attention. He continued to run toward the entrance of the mine. As he came around the bend where he could see out of the mine, he stopped abruptly and stared out of the mine.

Standing on the ground in front of the mine entrance was that same large Golden Eagle. The eagle was looking right at Wilber, and he didn't look very friendly. Wilber reached for his gun, but it wasn't there. He had apparently lost it when he panicked and ran in the mine. Wilber didn't know what to do. He was sure that there was a ghost behind him, and a very large, angry eagle in front of him. He could hear only two things, the sound of George's pleas for him to come back, and the screaming of an angry eagle as it spread its wings and pounded its feet on the ground.

"Wilber, where are you? I can't see a thin' in here. Come back," George called out from the darkness, but he got no answer.

Wilber was afraid to answer George. He was sure that the eagle would attack him if he made any noise or moved.

When George didn't get a reply from Wilber, he started to slowly move along the mine tunnel toward the entrance. He kept one hand on the side of the tunnel wall. With each small step he took, the fear of tripping and falling ran through his mind. The thought that he might end up wandering aimlessly in the darkness consumed his mind, and he began to sweat. If he got lost in the dark, he might fall in a hole or make a wrong turn in the tunnel or hit his head on something. He began to think that he might die lost and alone in the mine.

It wasn't long before George's mind was playing all sorts of tricks on him. He began to panic when he heard the whispery voice again. It sounded as if it was only a few feet behind him. He turned suddenly, but could see nothing. He drew his gun and fired a couple of shots into the darkness. He heard the voice again, but it sounded like it was behind him. He swung around and fired several more shots until his gun was empty, but he kept on hearing the voice. It seemed to make no difference which way he turned, the voice was always behind him. George had turned so many times that he lost all sense of direction. He had no idea which way to go to get out of the mine. He was in a dark, cold place where he couldn't even see his hand in front of his face.

"Wilber! Wilber! Please, Wilber, help me," he pleaded, but there was no answer.

Wilber stood close to the entrance of the mine. He was afraid to go back for George and afraid to go out with the eagle standing there staring at him. Suddenly, the large eagle took flight and disappeared from sight. Wilber let out a sigh of relief now that the eagle was gone. He took a step toward the entrance, then stopped. He realized that he had not seen where the eagle had gone. It could have gone up above the entrance and was waiting for him to come out. Would the eagle attack him if he tried to leave the mine? What would the eagle do to him?

Suddenly, Wilber heard the sound of footsteps outside the mine. He moved up against the side of the tunnel. Was the old man's ghost coming to get him?

"Please, mister, please, don't kill me," Wilber whined.

"I ain't going to kill you," the whispery voice said from behind a rock. "You come out of the mine with your hands in the air and you just might live."

Wilber wasn't sure what to do. If he walked out of the mine, would the old man shoot him? Would the eagle attack him? What choice did he have but to do as he was told?

"I'm coming out."

Setting the lamp down on the ground, he put his hands in the air and slowly walked out of the mine. As he came out into the light, he could see the old man behind a rock with a rifle pointing at him. Wilber couldn't help himself. He had to look up above the entrance to see if the eagle was up there. He slowly turned and looked up. Wilber quickly dropped to his knees and covered his head with his hands at the sight of the eagle perched on a rock above the entrance looking down at him.

"I see you're a mite bit scared of my friend. He don't take kindly of strangers goin' in his mine. Now lay flat on the ground. Don't move and he won't hurt you."

Wilber did as he was told. The old man took a rope and tied him up. He then took Wilber over to a tree and secured him to it.

"I think your friend could use a little help gettin' out of my mine."

"Don't leave me with that eagle," Wilber pleaded.

"You just sit tight and he won't hurt you."

The old man started into the mine. He took the coal lamp and slowly started down the tunnel. It wasn't long before he found George curled up on the tunnel floor crying like a baby, trembling with fear and mumbling something about a ghost. It was not the first time the old man had seen that happen to a man who found himself in complete darkness with no sense of direction.

"It's time to get out of here," the old man said as he stood near George.

George slowly turned his head and looked up at the old man. At first he thought he was seeing a ghost and covered his face with his hands.

"Please don't hurt me," he cried.

"Come on. I'll help you out of here."

George looked up at the old man again. Slowly, George stood up. It was when he was standing up that he saw the gun in the old man's hand.

"Let's go," the old man said as he pointed his gun in the direction he wanted George to go.

George's face was streaked from the tears of fear that ran down his face. He moved rather slowly and continued to mumble something about ghosts. He had never felt such fear in all his life.

When they came out of the mine, George heard the screeching of the eagle. It sent a cold chill down his spine. It was as if the bird was announcing the victory of the old man and the eagle over the evil men.

The old man tied George up to a tree next to Wilber. He then turned and looked at the eagle. The old man saluted the eagle, smiled, then watched the big bird fly off across the valley.

After the bird had flown away, the old man went over to George and Wilber. He looked down at them. He couldn't help but think they were the most pathetic souls he had ever seen. Wilber had been so frightened by the eagle that he kept looking toward the sky. George was shaking all over and mumbling about ghosts.

The old man found their horses. He tied them in the saddle and took them out of the mountains to the nearest town. He handed them over to the town marshal. After the marshal put them in a jail cell, he just looked at the two men, then looked at the old man.

"I never saw two men that were so willin' to go to jail," the marshal said.

"I hope you can get somethin' out of them," the old man said with a grin.

After explaining to the marshal what had happened to them, the old man left town. It was a long trek back to his mine.

When he returned to his mine in the mountains, the old man began rebuilding his cabin where he lived out his days in peace, never seeing either of the two men again. As for the eagle, it kept the old man company for many years.

ENCOUNTERS ON THE FRONITER

It was early September of 1855 when Joshua Higgins found himself slowly plodding across the vast open prairie west of the Missouri River. The weather was hot and dry with a warm breeze blowing in from the southwest. The buffalo grass that covered the prairie was brown and dry. It crunched under Joshua's feet as he pulled his two-wheel cart across the land. He had built the cart with fairly large wheels so that it would roll over the ruts and rocks with ease.

As Joshua moved across the plains, he kept a watchful eye out for any danger that might befall him. He was pulling his cart down the long slop of a hill toward a river. When he got to the river, he found that it was like many small prairie rivers during the late summer and early fall, very shallow. It was hardly more than ankle deep where he wanted to cross.

Once he was on the other side, he pulled his cart in among the large old cottonwood trees that grew close to the river. He decided it would be a good place to spend the night before he continued on west over the hill.

Joshua knew that he would have to be very careful about building a fire as he had seen Indians earlier in the day. It could not have much smoke because it could be seen for miles from the tops of the hills on both sides of the river. He found a lot of small branches that would make a good fire.

Staying close to his cart, he cleared an area large enough to build a small fire. Once he had his fire, he began cooking his evening meal and making himself a cup of coffee. He kept his eyes moving and his Kentucky long rifle close at hand. He also kept his pistol tucked in his belt where it would be handy if he should need it in a hurry.

As darkness started to fill the valley, he let his fire burn down to coals. He got his bedroll and spread it out on the ground close to the cart. Joshua put his rifle and English made single shot pistol in the cart under the tarp to keep the morning dew off them. They would be no use to him if the powder was damp.

Joshua then sat down and leaned back against the wheel of his cart. He took a few minutes to listen to the sounds of the night. He wanted to get used to the sounds of the breeze in the trees, the sounds of the water in the river as it flowed over the rocks and the sounds of the animals as they were all a part of the night. That way if he heard a strange sound he would know that something was not right.

It wasn't long before Joshua knew what to listen for. He laid down on his bedroll next to his cart and looked up at the sky. Even after sleeping under the stars for many weeks, he still couldn't get over how big the sky looked on a clear night. After watching the stars for a little while, Joshua closed his eyes and drifted off to sleep.

* * * *

Joshua woke as the sun was coming up over the ridge on the east side of the river. The soft grass in among the large cottonwood trees and the sounds of the night had given him a very peaceful and restful night's sleep. It was the first time in many nights that it had been cool enough to get a good night of rest. Up until now, the nights had been almost as hot as the days.

Still lying on his bedroll, he stretched to loosen the stiffness in his muscles before sitting up. He rubbed the sleep from his eyes then began to look around. He stopped suddenly, freezing in place at the sight of eight young Indian braves sitting on their ponies and looking at him. They were only about fifteen feet away from him in sort of a half circle just looking at him. Joshua wasn't sure what he should do. He had never encountered Indians before.

The Indians didn't know what to make of the strange looking man lying on a blanket. They were rather curious about the white man. They had never seen a white man with a two-wheel cart that he pulled himself. The white men they had seen before had always had horses or wagons to carry their supplies, and they had only seen them at a distance.

Joshua looked at the braves. All of them were dark skinned and appeared to be very strong. They wore nothing but a loincloth and moccasins. Each of them had a single eagle feather in their hair. There was also a single eagle feather in the mane of each of their horses. They all had a bow hung over their shoulder and a quiver full of arrows. They carried knives in their belts. One of the braves also carried a long sharp lance that he held firmly in one hand. The lance had several small clumps of hair attached to it. Joshua was not sure if it was human hair or not.

None of the young warriors were wearing war paint on their faces, which was a bit of a relief to Joshua. However, the expressions on their faces gave Joshua no hint of how they felt about seeing him on their hunting grounds. He had no idea what they were intending to do.

Joshua's first thought was to grab his rifle from the cart to defend himself, but his rifle was under the tarp and would not be easy to retrieve. Even if he did get one of his guns, they could easily kill him before he could reload.

The one thing that eased Joshua's feelings about them was the young braves didn't seem to be threatening him. Joshua decided to take a chance and stand up. He slowly stood up and faced them.

Joshua tried not to show that he was afraid. Not sure what he should do, he decided to raise his hand in a gesture of friendship. He could only hope they took the gesture in the manner that it was meant. He raised his hand, but the braves simply looked at him as if they didn't know what it meant.

Since his gesture had not drawn a response, he decided to try something else. He put his fingers tips of one hand together and raised his hand to his mouth in the hope that he was asking them if they wanted something to eat. The braves looked at each other, then turned and looked at him, but didn't say anything.

After a moment or so, the brave with the spear nodded slightly. Joshua wasn't sure what the status of the young brave was in the tribe, but he seemed to be the leader.

Joshua motioned for them to get down off their ponies and sit down around the place where he had had his fire. Again they looked at each other as if they were not sure if getting down was a good idea. Finally, the brave who had nodded at Joshua swung his leg over his pony's neck and gracefully slid off the back of the pony. He stood on the ground next to his pony for a moment or two before walking toward Joshua.

The young brave then turned and motioned for the rest of the braves to join him. The rest of the braves got off their ponies, but none of them sat down.

After the leader sat down, Joshua turned his back to him and reached into the cart. It was only after he had turned his back to them that he remembered the advice he had gotten from an old man he had met in Omaha. The old man had told Joshua that he should never turn his back on an Indian. Joshua didn't really have a choice if he wanted to feed them. All the food Joshua had was in his cart which was behind him when he was facing the Indians.

Joshua took a deep breath, then reached under the tarp on the cart. He only hoped that they would not think he was going for a weapon. Joshua pulled out a slab of salt pork wrapped in a cloth. Without turning back around, he unwrapped the salt port, took the knife from his belt and cut several thick slices from the slab. He placed the meat in a fry-pan.

Leaving the pan on the back of the cart, Joshua turned around. He was going to restart his fire, but was surprised to see the young brave was starting the fire for him. The young brave understood enough to know that Joshua was offering them something to eat, and a fire would be needed to cook it.

Joshua smiled at the young brave, nodded his approval of what the brave was doing and then reached under the tarp for his coffee pot. He motioned for the others to join the young brave at the fire. Reluctantly, the others sat down around the fire.

As soon as the Indians were sitting around the fire, Joshua took another big risk. He took his coffee pot down to the river and filled it with water. He could feel their eyes on him every step of the way. He had turned his back on them again. It made him very nervous; but by being polite and offering them a sign of friendship, it might keep them from killing him.

After filling the coffee pot with water, he returned to the fire. Again they watched him walk back to the fire. They never seemed to take their eyes off him, which was a little nerve-racking to Joshua.

Joshua put coffee in the pot and put it on the fire. While it was brewing, he retrieved the fry-pan from the cart, put it over the fire and began cooking the salt pork.

The Indians seemed to understand what he was doing. It wasn't until Joshua reached for his knife to turn the salt pork over in the fry-pan that there was a problem. When he reached for his knife, every one of the Indians reached for their knives. Joshua froze as he looked at them. He knew he had made a gesture that they did not understand. Joshua didn't move for a moment or two while looking at them.

After several tense moments, Joshua slowly removed his knife from his belt. Very slowly, he leaned toward the fry-pan. He stuck the point of his knife into a piece of salt pork and slowly turned it over. When the braves saw what he was doing, they took their hands away from their knives and relaxed. Joshua let out a sigh of relief and smiled at the braves. The braves continued to watch his every move as Joshua finished preparing breakfast for them.

Once the coffee was ready and the meat was done, they started to eat. When the food and coffee were gone, Joshua sat looking at them. He wasn't sure what to do next.

After they had their fill, the leader stood and the others did the same. When Joshua stood, the leader handed Joshua the empty cups, nodded slightly and smiled. He then watched them as they rode off. He wondered where they were going as they rode back across the shallow river and headed east.

As soon as they were out of sight, he packed up his belongings and began his trek west. For the next few days the only living things he saw were a few jackrabbits, lots of prairie dogs, several small herds of antelope and a few birds of which there were only a couple that he could identify. He had not seen a single person.

* * * *

On the forth day after his first encounter with Indians, Joshua was meandering along an old buffalo trail that led toward a small grove of trees on the bank of a narrow river. It was the first shade he had seen in a long time. The small group of trees along the river bank looked like it would be a cool place for him to spend a quiet and restful night. He could hardly wait to get in the shade of the trees and rest.

As Joshua moved closer to the large trees, he began to wonder if he would ever see his new friends again. His thoughts were suddenly disturbed by yelling and screaming. He looked off to his left and saw nine warriors as they came galloping down the long hill.

It quickly became clear they were not looking or acting very friendly. He quickly realized that he was in trouble if he didn't get to some cover. He started running down the hill toward the trees. He pulled his two-wheel cart as fast as he could. The Indians were on horses and were gaining on him very fast. It was a race to save his life.

Joshua had no more than gotten to the trees when he grabbed his rifle from the cart. He ran around the cart, putting it between him and the charging Indians. He knew that the cart would provide him with only a small measure of protection while he tried to defend himself, but it was better than nothing. Joshua jerked his rifle up to his shoulder and took aim at the warrior closest to him. He fired his Kentucky long rifle. The ball from his rifle hit the young warrior nearest to him square in the chest. The Indian went flying off his horse and hit the ground hard in a cloud of dust.

Joshua didn't have time to reload the rifle. He quickly dropped his rifle onto the cart and drew his pistol from his belt. He fired it at another warrior who was trying to turn his horse while looking for a place to take cover. The slug from Joshua's pistol caught the second warrior in the upper left side of his chest. The warrior spun around and fell from his horse hitting the ground only a few yards from the cart. The warrior turned over, then stopped moving.

The remaining warriors quickly retreated to a shallow gully about two hundred to two hundred and fifteen yards from the grove of trees. In a matter of a few seconds, Joshua had reduced their numbers to seven. It was clear that when he tried to run from them, they had not expected him to turn on them and kill two of them so quickly. If nothing else, he made them more cautious about attacking him again.

While the warriors tried to regroup in the gully and plan their next move, Joshua reloaded both his pistol and his rifle. He readied himself for another attack which he was sure would be coming soon. He laid out his powder and shot within easy reach so that he could load his weapons fast. He was hoping that if they charged him, he could get at least two shots off with his rifle. That way he could save his pistol for when they got in close.

Once he was ready, he waited. There was no way for him to tell what they would do next. He had surprised them, that was a good thing for him. Another good thing was he had his cart. He had everything in his cart that he would need to put up a fight. Even so, seven against one were not the best odds.

Joshua began to look around at where he found himself. He was fairly close to the river, and he had some cover from the trees in the small grove. He thought his position among the trees was good, but he could make it a little better if he dragged his cart closer to the river where a very large cottonwood tree had fallen. It would make it easier for him to see his enemy if they should try to circle around and attack him from the river. He put his cart close to the dead tree.

The one thing he knew he would need was water. The grass along the narrow bank of the river was fairly tall. If he was careful, he could crawl down to the river after dark and fill his canteens with water. But for now there was nothing for him to do but wait and see what the warriors were going to do, and wait until dark. He was hoping they would give it up and leave, but seriously doubted that was going to happen.

As Joshua looked around, he heard something hit one of the trees about five feet away. It was quickly followed by the sound of a rifle shot. He had not noticed that one of the Indians had a rifle. He looked for a sign of where the shot had come from. He could see the smoke from the gun as it slowly drifted away. It gave him a good idea where the Indian was who had fired the shot.

The Indian who had fired the shot was a good distance away. It seemed to Joshua that the Indian was not a very good marksman. He thought the Indian was probably not very familiar with a rifle, and it gave Joshua the advantage. Joshua also had the advantage because he was used to shooting long distances. He was about to show the Indian that a gun was of little use if he didn't know how to use it. He laid his rifle over the top of his cart and took aim at where the Indian had shot from. He waited. When the Indian stuck his head up and tried to take careful aim at Joshua, Joshua fired. His shot hit its mark just as the Indian fired. The Indian's shot went into the dirt about twelve feet too short and to the right of Joshua, while Joshua's shot hit the Indian hard on his right shoulder. He didn't think that he had killed the Indian, but he was sure he had taken him out of the fight.

After the exchange of rifle fire, it was quiet again. There were no more attempts to fire the rifle by any of the Indians. Joshua was not sure if it was because none of the other Indians knew how to shoot it, or if they had decided the rifle was of little use to them. The Indian probably had a saddle rifle which was a fairly short range rifle. It was nothing like the long range rifle Joshua carried.

Time drifted by very slowly. The warriors seemed content to wait and watch him. Every once in a while he could see an Indian pop his head up and look toward him, but that was all. They were too far away to hit him with an arrow. Even so, it became clear they had no intentions of leaving. They were planning something. The only question was what? As long as it was light it would be hard for them to get closer to him. He wondered if they would wait until dark and then move in closer.

As darkness fell upon the land, Joshua could hear the wild animal calls of the warriors. It was very unsettling. He had no one to help him keep watch so that he could get a little sleep. Several times Joshua dozed off only to wake up at the sound of an animal call made by the Indians. Maybe it was their plan to keep him awake and tire him so he would not have a clear head in the morning when it came time to fight back, he thought.

It suddenly occurred to Joshua that if he could use the tall grass to get to the river for water, the Indians could use it to sneak up on him. He began to think it might be better if he were to try to escape rather than stay and fight. After all, he was outnumbered. If the river was deep enough, he could swim out into the river and float on downstream until he was far enough away to be out of danger. Joshua knew that he would have to leave his cart and most of his supplies behind.

Joshua began to select just those things he would need everyday to survive and put them in his backpack. He saved one tin cup, some hardtack, a little coffee, a canteen and his field glasses along with a few other things that he would need like his bedroll, powder and shot. He wrapped his powder in oil cloth to keep it dry. Since his backpack was made of hides, it would help keep things inside dry if he was not in the water too long. He kept his pistol and rifle where he could reach them.

As soon as he had everything he would need sealed in his backpack, he crawled down to the river's edge. He moved as quietly as possible. When he got to the river, he found the current of the river was fairly slow which led him to believe that it might be deep enough to swim in.

He thought about floating downstream to escape, but his enemy might be waiting for him downstream. Joshua decided to go upstream even though it would be harder.

Joshua crawled out into the water. He found it was deep enough that he could stand up with just his head and shoulders out of water. He floated his backpack ahead of him. Joshua held his pistol and rifle tightly on top of the backpack to keep them dry. He moved slowly and carefully. One slip and he would not only give away his escape, but he could loose his balance and dump his rifle and pistol in the river. At best, it would make them useless until he dried them out. At worst, he could lose them in the darkness. Either way, he would not have anything to fight with except his knife.

Time passed slowly as Joshua pushed his backpack upstream. The sky was full of stars, but there was no moon. It made it very dark and almost impossible to see anything that was more than a few feet away. As he moved along in the river, he could hear the occasional wild animal calls of the Indians gradually fade as the distance grew between him and his enemy.

Joshua continued to move upstream. Moving against the current made it tough going. He was beginning to feel the cold of the water. It was making his body ache. He knew that he had little choice but to keep moving.

Joshua had no idea how far he had gone when he began to see the eastern sky start to show signs that morning was coming. He had to find someplace to hide where they could not find him. There was little or no cover except for the tall grass at the very edge of the river. If he left the river, he would not only be out in the open, but it would not be difficult for the Indians to discover where he left the river and follow him. He kept looking for someplace to hide as he continued to move up stream.

In the faint morning light, he noticed a fairly large area of cattails that looked like they went back into a narrow draw. There was probably a creek or small stream that flowed into the river from behind the cattails. He decided the cattails would provide a good place to hide until he was sure the Indians had given up hunting him.

Joshua worked his way toward the cattails until the water was to shallow to continue to keep low in it. He stood up and tucked his pistol in his belt, then took his rifle in one hand and his backpack in the other. Joshua waded through the shallow water and mud into the cattails.

He worked his way in among the cattails. He had to be very careful to make sure he didn't break off any of the cattails, or leave any sign of where he had gone. He made sure he could not be seen by anyone nearby.

Once inside the stand of cattails, Joshua discovered a large rock that would provide him with a place where he could set his backpack and get himself out of the cold water. When he was seated on the rock, the tall cattails still rose well above his head. He rested his rifle on his backpack while he took a few minutes to catch his breath.

He was wet and cold from being in the water so long. Now it was time to wait and hope that the Indians would not find him and give up the search.

The sun slowly came up over the horizon and began to warm him. It felt good, but he was hungry. He had not eaten since yesterday morning. He had left most of his food. He had only a little coffee and a few hardtack biscuits. Joshua thought about starting a small fire and brewing some coffee in his metal cup. A cup of hot coffee would help warm him, but he knew it was too risky to build a fire. Any smoke from a fire would certainly draw attention to where he was hiding. For now, he would have to let the sun warm him and dry his clothes.

Time passed slowly. His clothes were slowly drying in the warm sun. He closed his eyes and wished that he had a place large enough to lie down so he could get some sleep. The rock was just barely large enough to provide a place to set his backpack and still leave him with enough room to sit so he could be out of the water.

Suddenly Joshua heard the sound of horses galloping along the bank of the river. He grabbed up his rifle and readied himself. He slowly stood up until his head was just above the cattails. He could see two Indians coming toward him. They were riding along the bank of the river looking for some sign of where he might have come out of the water. He quickly ducked down.

Since there were only two Indians, he figured that some of the others had gone downstream from where he had left his cart. He thought about rising up again to see if there were any Indians on the other side of the river, but he didn't dare. Those on his side of the river were too close and might see him.

Joshua kept his head down and listened for any sound that would indicate they were going to search the cattails. He could hear the sound of horses wading in the shallow water around the edge of the cattails. It was obvious they were looking for a sign that he might be hiding in among them.

Joshua mentally prepared himself for a fight. There was no doubt in his mind it would be a fight for his life. He held his rifle in his hands as his eyes searched for any movement among the cattails that were close to him. Joshua could feel his heart pounding in his chest and sweat run down his face as he waited and listened.

The Indians were so close to him that he could hear them talking. Joshua didn't understand very much of what they were saying, but it was clear they were not sure where he went. He was ready for a fight as he waited to see if they might come into the cattails looking for him.

After what seemed like an eternity, Joshua heard the sounds of horses running off. The Indians were headed back in the direction they had come. Joshua let out a sigh of relief and set his rifle on top of his pack. They had probably decided that he was no longer worth the effort it would take to find him.

As soon as it was quiet, Joshua thought about getting out of the cattails, but didn't move. He was not sure if what he had heard was them leaving or a ploy to get him to show himself. He decided to wait until the sun was directly overhead before he felt that it would be safe to move.

Convinced that the Indians had given up their search for him, he gathered his belongings and slowly started working his way out of the cattails. Once Joshua was out of the cattails, he took a look around. He could not see anyone in any direction.

His decision to move north still seemed like a good idea. Joshua could see no reason to go back for his supplies. He figured there would be very little left once the raiding party had finished with it.

Joshua began moving north. At least for the next couple of miles, he would keep an eye to the south just in case the raiding party came back his way. While looking south, he noticed a thin column of smoke off in the distance. He climbed up a hill to get a better look. When he reached the top of the ridge, he could see that there was something burning and it appeared to be near the river. It was several miles away. Although he could not see what was burning, he was sure the raiding party had taken out their frustration of not finding him by setting his cart on fire and destroying everything he had they could not use.

Joshua watched the smoke rise up from the river valley for several minutes. He gave out a sigh, then turned and headed north.

A TOWN IS BORN

The wind was blowing out of the northwest across the wide open prairie of the Dakota Territory. East of the Missouri River there had been plenty of rich grass and slow moving streams. At the Missouri River there had been lots of wood for fires from the many cottonwood trees. The trees also provided plenty of shade along the banks of the river while the river provided plenty of water for the weary travelers and their livestock.

Crossing the river had been difficult for both man and beast. A raft was built to float the wagons and the oxen across the river. It took two days to build the raft and another two days to get everyone across.

Once across the river, the large oxen, eight to a wagon, strained to pull the heavily laden covered wagons up the long gentle grade leading west away from the Missouri River. The ten wagons were strung out as they moved slowly along the hard ground, each one stirring up small clouds of dust from the dry parched land.

The small group of travelers pushed on toward the Black Hills. Outriders kept an eye out for any kind of danger that might fall upon the wagon train as it slowly worked its way west.

The wagon train was only three days away from where it had crossed the Missouri River. The country had changed a great deal in that short time. West of the river the land quickly turned dry and wind blown. Now there was nothing but buffalo grass on the otherwise barren land. The buffalo grass was dry from a lack of rain, and crunched under the wheels of the heavy wagons. It was hard to find a single tree within miles. The land was full of gullies and ravines that were dry, except when it rained. It hadn't rained for weeks. The gullies and ravines made it difficult for the animals to pull the heavy wagons.

Out on the open plains it seemed as if the wind blew every day and every night making travel extremely uncomfortable. The land promised the small band of dreamers nothing but growing hardships with each mile they traveled further away from the Missouri River and its life-giving water. Their only hope was that life would be better once they got to the Black Hills where there was the promise of flowing streams, green grasses and timber to build houses, barns and businesses.

As the days passed, the small band of adventurers continued to move west making only ten to twelve miles a day, on a good day. Conditions seemed to get worse with each passing day and each passing mile. Water had to be rationed, and buffalo dung had to be gathered wherever it could be found to use in place of firewood. The heat of the day and the dust blowing almost constantly made some of the members of the small band of travelers lose sight of their goals, and some of them to lose their faith, while some of them simply lost hope.

But those were not the only problems they would face. There were many dangers in crossing the plains. One of the many dangers they faced showed up just two weeks after crossing the Missouri River.

The wagon train was strung out and moving slowly across the wind blown plains. Most of the women and children were walking alongside the wagons while the men coaxed the oxen along.

Suddenly, one of the outriders came racing across the dry hard prairie. He seemed to be yelling something, but Jacob French, their leader and guide, couldn't understand him. Jacob stopped the lead team of oxen and waited until the outrider got closer.

"Indians! Indians!" the outrider yelled.

Jacob knew they didn't have time to gather the wagons into a circle. The oxen were not an animal that could be rushed. At best they could get them to close up the distance between them. He could see the Indians coming over the hill behind the outrider.

"Close up, close up. Woman and children get in the wagons" he said as he yelled out instructions.

"All men take cover under the wagons and be ready to fight."

The message was quickly spread along the wagon train. Men quickly tossed their children into the wagons and grabbed up their rifles. The women were climbing into the wagons and gathering the weapons that would be needed to fend off the attack.

As the outrider reined in his horse, he jumped off with his rifle in his hands. He quickly scrambled under a nearby wagon. He had no more than readied himself for the fight when the shooting began. The air filled with the smell of burnt gunpowder and the loud noise of gunfire.

Only a few of the Indians had rifles, but the shear number of them charging down the hill filled the small band of pioneers with fear. The Indians yelling and their painted faces added to the pioneers fear.

It had all started very quickly, leaving everyone no time to think about what was taking place. There was confusion everywhere. The battle lasted only a few minutes before the Indians turned and retreated back over the hill. The Indians had been outmatched in firepower, if not in numbers.

The men continued to lay under the wagons to watch and wait for another attack. It seemed like they waited forever, but after only a few minutes they began to crawl out from under the wagons. They looked at each other as if they didn't understand what had just happened.

Slowly, the men began to look around while still keeping a sharp eye out in case the Indians tried another attack. Once it appeared they were not going to be attacked again, Jacob started looking around. He began to appraise the damage.

The first thing Jacob noticed was that several of the oxen were down. But it wasn't until he began walking down the line of wagons that he saw three of the men had been wounded. He saw the women were quick to respond and had begun caring for the injured men.

When he got to the last wagon, he found Martha McCullen sitting on the ground. She had her husband's head in her lap and she was crying. As Jacob approached her, she looked up at him. Tears were running down her face.

It was clear the attack had taken her husband's life.

Jacob looked back up the line of wagons. The three men who were injured would need care, and Frank McCullen would have to be buried. Jacob began to give orders to the members of the wagon train.

"Those of you who can, cut the dead and wounded oxen loose. Then hook up the rest to the wagons and pull them around into as small a circle as you can. Tie the oxen that are left to the wagons inside the circle. We will have to spend the night here."

"We have to get out of here," Sally Sutton said, her voice showing how scared she was of another attack. "We can't stay here. The savages will come back."

Sally was almost in a state of panic. Jacob walked up to her, put his arms around her and held her tightly against him. He could understand her wanting to get away, everyone wanted to get away. Her husband was one of the men who had been wounded in the attack, but he would survive. His injuries were not so severe that they were life threatening.

"Listen," he said softly. "Listen to me. We are better off staying right here for now, than to start moving again. If they see that we are better prepared, they may decide not to attack us again. If we are spread out, it will make it easier for them to do us harm."

"But I don't want to stay here."

"I know, but believe me, it is better for us to stay here for a day or two, than to be caught spread out," Jacob said as he smiled a reassuring smile.

"I guess maybe you're right," Sally said, finally conceding as she looked up at him.

"Now do what you can to help get things in order. Okay?"

"Okay," she replied then turned to see what she could do to help.

Jacob watched her as she walked off toward the Sutton wagon to care for her husband. He then turned and walked over toward a couple of the men who were working on cutting the dead oxen from their harnesses.

"Skin the oxen that are dead and shoot the ones that are so badly injured they are useless to us. Have the women prepare as much of the meat as they can for travel." Jacob said.

"There's more meat here than we can use," Joseph Martin said to Jacob. "It will spoil before we can use it. What do we do with it?"

"Drag the oxen carcasses out away from the wagons toward where the Indians came from. Maybe they will take them and leave us alone."

The men went right to work on a couple of the oxen, while the outrider began dragging a couple of the oxen out away from the wagons. One of the men and a couple of the woman prepared a grave for Frank McCullen. Since there were no trees in the area, and they didn't have any spare wood to make a casket, Martha took one of the quilts she had made and wrapped her husband in it.

Jacob stood by Martha as they buried her husband. He put his arm around her to comfort her while Joseph read a few words from the Good Book. After Frank was put in the grave and the grave had been filled in, Jacob walked Martha to her wagon.

"There are things I need to do. Will you be all right?"

"Yes," Martha said as she looked up at Jacob. "I need a little time alone, anyway. Thank you."

Jacob nodded slightly then turned to do what needed to be done. Jacob immediately began to take assessment of the situation. They would need no less than four oxen to move a wagon, but that would be if they didn't have any steep hills to go over. Six per wagon would be better, but even then it would be difficult for the animals. Jacob felt it might be better for the animals if they lightened up the wagons by leaving everything that was not absolutely necessary behind.

Leaving their personal belongings behind was going to mean some very hard decisions would have to be made by everyone. Many of them had pieces of furniture that had been in their families for many years and meant a great deal to them.

The small band of travelers worked hard doing those things that had to be done. They circled the wagons to form a more secure place to fight from if necessary. They put the oxen that were able to pull the wagons inside the circle to make sure they were safe for the night. When the animals were secure, they helped look after the wounded men.

As night spread out over the land, the small band of travelers gathered around the evening fire in the center of the circle. Since some of them had lost their faith and their dreams of a future in the Black Hills, a few of them began talking quietly about going back. Finally one of them spoke up for all to hear. It was Wilber Johnson.

"I think we should turn around and go back. I, for one, was not expecting to be set upon by Indians," Wilber said with a hint of anger in his voice.

"You were told what to expect out here. We all were," Joseph Martin reminded him.

"I didn't figure on there being so many Indians."

"What would you have us do?" Ralph Swenson asked. "You think we should turn back? Back to what? Every one of us here sold everything we had in order to make this journey,"

"May I say something?" Martha McCullen asked.

"Sure," Joseph said politely.

"My husband and I had sold off everything we had to move out west."

"We know that. So did the rest of us," Wilber said interrupting her.

"Give her a chance to have her say," Joseph said. "Everyone will get their chance to speak."

"Thank you, Joseph," Martha said before she continued. "Frank and I were planning on opening a general store when we found a place to build the store and settle in. I still want to do that."

"And who will run the store?" Wilber asked in a sarcastic way.

"I will," Martha said rather sharply. "I can run a general store as well as anyone."

"So, you still want to go on. Is that what you are saying?" Joseph asked.

"No. Not really."

"What do you mean?" Jacob asked wondering what she had in mind.

"After we crossed the Missouri River, Frank was saying that he thought the place we crossed would have been a good place to build our general store, and maybe start a town," Martha continued.

Everyone sat there looking at each other and trying to understand what she was saying. Even several of the women began talking to their husbands about the idea.

Jacob had been hired to lead the small band of travelers to the Black Hills. But the talk he was hearing was that maybe they had already gone further than they really wanted to go.

"Frank said there was good rich farm land on the east side of the river. He also said that there was plenty of land for those who wanted to ranch. He said we could build a town near the river. The river would provide a way to get our goods out to other markets, and it would provide a way to get goods to us," Martha said.

"That's all well and good for you. But what about the rest of us?" Wilber asked.

"Frank thought of you, too," she said as she looked at Wilber and smiled. "His idea was that once the area for the town had been selected and was laid out, each family would put their name on a piece of paper and put it in a hat, then each name would be drawn out of the hat one at a time. Each family would pick out a plot of land on which to build their farm or ranch based on a drawing of the land around the town. Since there are only six families who expressed an interest in ranching or farming, they could each front on the river and go back as far from the river as necessary to provide for what they wanted to do. It could even be set up with three families on one side of town and three on the other."

"That sounds like a good idea to me," Joseph Martin said as he looked around to see if there were any others who agreed with him.

"We would have to all get together and plan out roads so that everyone could get to town to sell what they wished, as well as to get some of the things they needed. That may mean some of you would have to allow roads to cross your land," Martha added. "But I don't think that would be a problem because we will all need roads to be able to move about anyway."

"What about the town? Will there be only the general store?" Anna Swenson asked.

"Maybe at first, but we could lay out the town so it would have room to grow," Martha said. "We could plot out the streets so that they are wide enough for freight wagons to turn around."

"Could we have a school?" Becky Martin asked hopefully.

"Yes. And a church," Martha added. "Maybe not all at once, but if we plan it right it could grow. Frank even said it could become a jumping off place for others who wanted to continue moving west, and someday maybe a place for river boats to stop."

"Jacob, what do you think?" Martha asked as she looked at him.

Jacob had been standing next to one of the wagons. He had been listening to everything that had been said. The one thing he noticed was that almost everyone seemed to be interested in the idea of going back to the

Missouri River and building a town. He thought about it, too, even if he did not join in the discussion. Now he was going to have to say something.

"I'm getting the feeling that at least most of you want to go back to the river and start a town close to where we crossed the river. I was hired by you folks to take you to the Black Hills. Now this brings up some questions."

"What kind of questions?" Walter wanted to know.

"What do I do if there are any of you who want to go on? Do I leave the rest of you to go back on your own while I take them on to the Black Hills. Or do I take the rest of you back and either let the ones that want to go on to the Black Hills go by themselves, or make them come back with you. I hope you can see where that puts me."

The families sitting around the fire began looking at each other. They had been doing a lot of talking, but it was becoming clear that some of the families wanted to talk over the idea of going back to the river among themselves.

"I see your point, Jacob," Joseph said. "Didn't you say that we would be here a day or two before we moved on?"

"Yes. I think it would be a wise thing to do. Besides the animals need some rest."

"Then I say we all call it a night," Joseph said. "That way we can talk it over with our family members, or whoever we want to talk it over with. Then we could meet around the fire at - say - noon tomorrow and find out who wants to go back to the river and who wants to go on."

"That sounds like a good idea to me. But for tonight, we need to stand watch. Women can stand watch, too. Stand watch for two hours at a time. I'll take the first watch with Joseph and ...." Jacob said, but was interrupted before he could finish.

"I'll stand watch," Martha said.

"Okay. Call out if you see or hear anything you're not sure about. The rest of you should try to get some sleep, but sleep with your guns close at hand."

The small group of travelers broke up and went to their wagons. As the evening wore on those standing guard could hear the others talking among themselves. It was not easy to hear what they were saying, but it was clear they were discussing the idea of going back to the river to settle down there and make it their home.

Martha had been standing guard for a little over an hour when Jacob walked over and stood beside her. She glanced over at him, but didn't say a word. She wondered what was on his mind.

"Is there something on your mind, Mr. French?"

"I was just wondering. Was the idea of a town really Frank's idea, or was it yours?" he asked in a whisper.

Martha looked at Jacob, then began to smile.

"It was mine. But it was Frank's idea to build a general store somewhere to supply the needs of people."

"I thought so," Jacob said with a smile.

"Frank and I were planning to build a general store in the Black Hills, but when I saw how nice it was along the shore of the Missouri River I thought it would be a nice place to build our store."

"I had thought a while back about giving up the job of leading wagon trains across the land," Jacob admitted. "I have been thinking about putting down roots somewhere. There are a lot of people who want to move west to look for riches, or just a new life. Why not help them by selling them the things they need and make a little money doing it?"

"I agree with you," Martha said with a smile.

"People traveling across this country will need a place to get supplies. I know what people will need." he said as he looked at her. "What better place to get what they need than at the river where they have to cross?"

"I heard you tell some of the men that the place we crossed was the best and easiest place to cross the river. I believe you said, "It is the best place to cross in thirty miles either way" from where we crossed. Was that true, or were you making it up?"

"It is true. In fact, it's more like fifty miles either way."

"Then what better place to build a business and a town?"

"None. You are one very smart woman," Jacob said. "We'll have to talk again in the morning."

"I would like that. Goodnight, Mr. French," Martha said with a smile.

"Goodnight, Martha."

Jacob turned and walked back to where he had laid out his bedroll for the night and lay down. He watched as Martha was relieved of her watch and walked across the circle to her wagon. When she disappeared inside the wagon, Jacob closed his eyes and went to sleep.

* * * *

When morning came, some of the older children took the remaining oxen out of the inner-circle of wagons to where they could feed on the dry buffalo grass. They stood watch over them in case they had to be moved back inside the circle in a hurry, and to keep them from wandering off.

The younger children, under the watchful eyes of some of the men, went outside the circle and gathered buffalo dung for the fire, then put it in the nets that hung under the wagons. Several of the women gathered around the fire in the center of the circled wagons and began preparing breakfast for everyone. A couple of the women took care of the three injured men making sure they were as comfortable as possible.

Once breakfast was finished and the morning chores had been done, the adults gathered around to discuss their future. Their future depended on whether they wanted to continue on to the Black Hills, or return to where they crossed the river to start a town or settle a ranch or farm. The first to speak was Jacob.

"First of all, we are gathered here to decide what we are going to do. Each family will be given a chance to express their opinion. But before we do that, I have a couple of things to say.

"As you saw yesterday, it is not just the weather, or the land that we have to deal with. The further we get away from the Missouri River, the more likely we are to have raiding parties attack us. You were all told that before we started.

"Water and feed for our livestock will be harder to find, as well. I have been over this trail several times, and not once did I get everyone across it safely. I have lost travelers to disease, Indian attacks, and to just some of the hardships that go with traveling across such wide open spaces.

"Now, that having been said, there are opportunities for anyone who will face the dangers of traveling across the prairie. There is some good land around the edge and in the Black Hills for farming and ranching. Although finding a large enough area to raise large herds of cattle in the Black Hills would be difficult. There are opportunities for those of you who wish to start a business if you are willing to work at it, and I mean, work hard at it.

"Each family must decide what they want. Do you want to go on and take your chances, or do you want to go back to the Missouri River and settle in the area where we crossed the river? Either way, there will be dangers, and there will be difficulties. That having been said, Anna Swensen asked me if she could speak for her family first. So we'll open our discussion with Anna Swenson, Anna."

"Ralph and I talked about it last night and again this morning."

"How is he doing?" Joseph asked, interrupting her.

"He is doing well. His injury was not severe. He should be up and around in a few days.

"As I was saying, we talked about it last night. He thinks it is a good idea for us to go back to the other side of the river. He could start a Blacksmith business and maybe have a livery stable in the town. People will need a good Blacksmith to make hinges, latches, shoes for horses, and all sorts of things made out of metal. He said that he could also deal in livestock from time to time if it was needed."

"So you vote to go back?" Jacob asked.

"Yes. Ralph and I would like to go back and start a business in the town," she said with a smile.

"Okay. What about you, Mrs. Sutton? Would you like to speak for your family?"

"Yes, Jacob. William and I vote to return to the Missouri River and settle there. As you can see from here William is sitting up next to our wagon and is doing fine. The injury to his leg should be better in a couple of days, and should heal just fine within a week or so. We want to ranch there."

"Wilber, would you like to speak now?"

"Yeah. We, that is the missus and me, ain't seen such good land fur farmin' like we seen back there on the other side of the river. We come from a place where 'bout the only thin' you could grow was rock. We'd like to go back and start us a farm along the river."

"Joseph, what do you say?"

"The missus and I talked about it, and we've decided we could have a real nice farm back at the river. We could raise vegetables for everyone. We vote for goin' back."

"What about you, Henry?"

"Well, I was thinkin' about goin' on ta them mountains called the Black Hills. But ya know, I could put tagether a pretty nice ranch over on the other side of the river. Who knows, I might find me a wife from one of them wagon trains passin' through," he said with a big grin.

Everyone had a good laugh. When the laughing died down, Jacob got everyone's attention again.

"We all know what Martha McCullen wants to do, unless she has changed her mind."

"I haven't, Jacob," she said.

The discussion continued until everyone had had a chance to express themselves. After everyone had their say, Jacob looked out over the group before he spoke.

"Okay, I guess that settles it."

"Not quite," Joseph said. "We ain't heard from you. You're part of this outfit. You've got a wagon. We know you was planning on staying in the Black Hills after this trip. What do you want to do? You want ta go back or go on?"

"I was hired by you people, so it's up to you."

"That ain't no answer, Jacob. What do you want to do?" Sally Sutton asked.

Jacob looked at Martha and saw her looking at him. He looked down at the ground for a moment, then looked up again.

"I'd like to go back and work at making a town on the east side of the Missouri River," he said with a grin.

"Well, I guess that settles it," Joseph said with a wide grin.

"I guess it does," Jacob said. "We go back to the river and cross back over it. We will spend the rest of today getting things organized so we can get everything back. We are short a few oxen, so it may be a little slow going."

"I've got just one question for Jacob," Joseph said. "I would like to know what you plan to do in our new town."

"Well, I was thinkin' about that last night. I have two ideas. I was thinking I just might like to open up a woodworking shop where I could make things out of wood and sell them."

"What kind of things, Jacob," Sally asked.

"When I was younger my father made furniture. I learned a lot about it and thought I could make furniture, cabinets and the like. Most things out of wood."

"What was the other thing," Martha asked.

"I was thinking I would start me a freight line. I could ship in the things we all needed and ship out things that we wanted to sell to others back east. Actually, I was thinking about doing both for awhile."

"That sounds great," Martha said smiling at him.

Jacob looked at Martha. She was smiling at him, but he wasn't sure why. She had just lost her husband. Was it possible that she was looking for someone to help her with the General Store? There was no doubt in his mind that Martha was a fine looking woman, and she was smart, too. It crossed his mind that she would make a fine looking wife.

The group broke up to get their wagons and animals ready to head back to the river. Several of the women got together and talked about what they would like to do once they got back on the other side of the river.

The next morning, the band of travelers began the journey back to the Missouri River. It took them a little over two weeks to get back to the river. When they arrived, they spent most of two days getting everyone across, using the same raft they used going west.

Once they were all across, they circled the wagons. Sitting around the fire in the center of the wagons, they began to discuss how to lay out the town. It was decided that the town should be built on the shore nearest the easiest place to cross the river.

Since there were six families who wanted to ranch or farm, it was decided that three families would ranch or farm on one side of town and three on the other. They agreed that Jacob should draw up a map to show how much land along the river each of the ranches or farms and the town would have. From the river, each ranch or farm could extend straight back as far as they wanted to go. Jacob was to have his map drawn up by noon the next day so all could see what it would look like. Then they all turned in for the night.

* * * *

The next morning, Jacob took a piece of paper and sketched out a plan for the entire group and for the layout of the town. When noon came around, everyone gathered for lunch and to look over the sketches. The sketch for the area covered seven miles along the bank of the river. The layout showed one mile in the middle for the town, and one mile for each farm or ranch. He had even sketched in where the roads would be.

The sketch of the town showed where the main road would come in from the east to the river. It also showed where the General Store might be located, and where the Blacksmith shop and livery stable, freight office and freight barn, and where other stores might be as the town grew. There were also places on the map for a church and a school. The rest of the town area was for homes.

As soon as everyone had had a chance to look over the sketches and they had finished their meal, they began to talk about the town. Everyone seemed to be excited about their new town.

"Martha and I had talked about how each family who wanted to ranch or farm would select their property. We would have a drawing. The first name drawn would be able to select the property they wanted first, and so on," Jacob said. "Is there any problem with that?"

"It sounds fair to me," Joseph said as he looked around to see if anyone disagreed.

From the sounds of it, everyone agreed.

"Okay," Jacob said. "Since Martha and I will not be drawing for any of the six farm or ranch properties, we thought it would be best if we did the drawing. Are there any objections?"

There were no objections.

"Okay. Martha and I wrote the name of the head of each of the six families that told us they were planning on ranching or farming on a piece of paper. They were all the same size and folded in the same way so everyone has an equal chance. Martha will draw the first one."

Martha reached in the hat that was held above her head and drew out a name. She gave the name to Jacob.

"The first choice of land goes to Wilber Johnson. What parcel of land do you want, Wilber?"

"Well, since I plan to farm and raise vegetables, I figure I should be close to town so I can sell them to Martha for her to sell to the rest of you."

Everyone had a good laugh before Wilber spoke again.

"I'd like that there parcel you've got marked as three. It's close to town and should be good for what the misses and I want."

"Okay," Jacob said then put Wilber's name over the parcel on the map.

Martha drew the next name. It was Franklin Miller. He chose parcel six since he planned to ranch. It would give him room to expand south and east since he had picked the one farthest from town.

The next name drawn was Henry O'Mare, he took parcel one, north of town to start his ranch.

As soon as all the parcels located out of town had been drawn, Jacob and Martha got together with the Swensens and Tim Randall to discuss where they wanted to put their businesses and homes.

Once that was settled, it was time to begin the building. Martha and Jacob worked together to build a general store first. The first one was fairly small as wood was hard to come by. They decided to build it so it could be used as a freight station as well, and so that it could be easily added to as needed.

The first few years were spent by each of the families building a place to live. It was only after that was done they began to build barns and other buildings on their property. By the time three years had passed several buildings had been built on the main street of the town. One of them was a hotel and bar that was built by Tim Randall. It only had six rooms to rent, but it was a real building.

Jacob made good money by freighting in boards from a lumber mill some hundred and fifty miles away. When he started doing that, things really began to bloom in the town. By the fall of the fourth year of the town, there was a bank, a hotel and saloon, a general store, a Blacksmith shop and livery stable, and even a saddle and boot makers shop.

Over time the town continued to grow. Many settlers stopped and didn't go any further. Some set up businesses, while others began to farm and ranch in the area, some on the other side of the river.

People met, got married and raised families. The town continued to grow. Even Henry found himself a wife from one of the wagon trains that passed through the town.

TROUBLE ON
MEDICINE MOUNTAIN

The notorious Baker gang had been robbing banks in the small towns in and around the Black Hills for well over a year. Although many a town sheriff had tried to catch them, they had always ended up losing the gang in the backcountry of the Black Hills.

The latest robbery took place in Hill City when the Baker gang robbed the tin mining company's payroll from the First Hill City Bank. The gang then headed south toward Custer.

A posse was quickly formed to chase them down. The gang had managed to lose the posse back in the hills west of Custer in the area called Hell's Canyon. When the posse returned to Hill City, it was disbanded and the men returned to their businesses and jobs. The local sheriff contacted the Territorial Marshal to ask for help.

Sam Gibbets, the Territorial Marshal, arrived in Hill City just five days after the robbery of the tin mining company's payroll. He rode up to the sheriff's office, stepped out of the saddle, tied his horse at the hitching rail and walked into the sheriff's office. After a brief greeting, they sat down to discuss the situation.

"We chased Baker and his gang west into the Hell's Canyon area where we lost them. It seems they were headed for Wyoming, probably to Newcastle, but we lost them before we got to the border. They headed into some pretty rough country."

"The Custer sheriff chased them into the same area a few months back and lost them there," Sam said. "But I don't think they would go to Newcastle."

"Why not?"

"They're wanted in Newcastle and a couple of them are pretty well known there. If what I have been hearing is correct, they may have a hideout somewhere near or on Medicine Mountain. They're just rumors, but I've heard enough of them to make me think there might be something to it."

"Why would they head south toward Custer if they have a hideout around Medicine Mountain?"

"Probably to get you and others to think they went into Wyoming. Hell's Canyon is rough country where it would be fairly easy to lose someone following them."

"What do you plan to do? You goin' up to Medicine Mountain?"

"I've been thinking about it. It has been their habit in the past to lay low for a couple of months before they hit another bank. If they are doing that, they have to have a place where they feel safe and comfortable; so they can relax and plan their next robbery."

"That's some pretty rough country up that way."

"Yeah, but that seems to be where they like it. I'm going to get some supplies and head up there tomorrow to look around."

"You goin' alone?"

"Yeah. It's less likely that they will spot me before I spot them. If I go alone, they aren't likely to think much of it."

"I wish you luck."

"I'll probably need a lot of it. Thanks."

Sam stood up, shook hands with the sheriff, then turned and left the sheriff's office. He led his horse down the street to the livery stable where he put his horse up for the night. He then went to the General Store and purchased what he thought he would need. When he had everything, he went to the boarding house for a good night's rest before he headed out after the Baker gang.

* * * *

The next morning, Sam Gibbets, headed for Medicine Mountain. He slowly began working his way through the thick forest along a trail that wound its way toward the mountain. When he got close to the base of the mountain, he swung off the trail.

After making sure he was not being followed, he began working his way around the base of the mountain toward the west side. As he rode slowly around the mountain, he kept an eye out for any tracks that might show him where someone had traveled.

Sam had been carefully scouring the area on the west side of the mountain for three days when he found some tracks on what looked like a deer trail. He had noticed there were tracks from several shod horses in among the deer tracks. He stopped and got down from his horse to examine the tracks in the dirt more closely. After examining the tracks so that he would recognize them if he saw them again, he slowly led his horse along the trail checking each hoof print. It wasn't long before he had discovered that six horses had used the deer trail.

Sam straightened up and looked at the trail that wound its way up the mountain as he thought about what he had found. The Baker gang consisted of six men, all hard, ruthless men capable of killing anyone who got in their way. Sam had no illusions about what he was getting into. One mistake and it might very well be his last.

Sam moved over to the side of his horse, put his foot in the stirrup and swung into the saddle. He nudged his horse in the ribs lightly and started up the trail. His horse slowly moved along the trail while Sam kept a sharp lookout for any danger. The trail was well covered with forest on both sides of him, making it difficult to see anyone who might be watching the trail.

As he rounded a fairly sharp turn in the trail, Sam reined up his horse. Just a few yards ahead the trail left the woods into the sunlight. He slowly moved closer to the edge of the woods and looked out into the open area. The trail became very narrow with a steep drop off on one side and a rocky slope formed by a rockslide on the other.

The rockslide was covered with loose shale that would make it very difficult, if not impossible, for a horse to climb. The shale would slip and slid under his horse's hooves. If he got off the trail by only a mere foot or so, his horse could slip and cause both of them to slide over the edge. To continue along the trail would also put Sam out in the open with no place to go for cover should he be attacked.

Remaining back in the woods, Sam sat in the saddle and looked out over the trail. He had to make a choice. One was to turn around, go back and try to find a way around the rockslide to the other side. The other was to take the chance of getting across the open area without being seen, and without his horse slipping on the loose shale.

The narrow trail across the shale was the perfect place to watch for someone coming up the mountain. It was also the perfect place for an ambush. Any sudden move by a horse or man could cause them to end up at the bottom of the drop off.

The marshal took a moment to look over the terrain while thinking about his options. He had not seen anything that would indicate there was anyone around or on the other side of the open area. Even so, he decided not to cross the open area, but would go back down the trail and try to work his way around the rockslide.

He backed his horse up a little, and then swung the horse around. Sam rode back down the trail a little ways, then stopped and stepped out of the saddle. He took his rifle from the scabbard in one hand, and the reins of his horse in the other. Being as quiet as possible, he led his horse off the trail and into the woods. Moving as quietly as possible through the woods, he worked his way up toward the top of the area of the rockslide. It was hard going, but he kept inside the woods where it would be difficult for anyone to see him.

When he reached the top of the rockslide, he tied his horse to a tree branch. Being very careful, he moved to the edge of the woods close to the edge of the rockslide. He looked out over the area where the shale covered the side of the hill. From his position, he could see almost the entire side of the mountain. The trail that ran across the shale rockslide was almost two hundred yards long before the trail disappeared into the woods again.

As he looked along the edge of the rockslide, he thought he saw something move just inside the woods about a hundred yards from where he was standing. Sam quickly ducked back deeper into the woods while still looking off toward where he had seen a movement. He knew that if he had been seen by Baker or any of his gang, they would be coming after him. It was time to get out of there.

Sam quickly returned to his horse, untied it and led it deeper into the woods. He moved further away from the rockslide. His horse made very little sound as it walked on the pine needles that covered the ground. He hadn't gone very far when he came to a place were there were a lot of trees that had been blown over in a strong wind and were lying on the ground. Some of them were very large. He carefully moved in among the fallen trees to a very large one.

He moved his horse around behind the fallen tree, then forced the horse down. He got the horse down on its side next to the tree, then laid down across its neck. He gently rubbed the horses head and face to keep it calm. The horse quickly settled down.

While Sam lay down on the horse, he could hear the sounds of someone walking to where the trees had fallen. It suddenly got very quiet. Sam laid without moving and listened, but didn't hear anything more for several minutes. It wasn't long before he heard someone.

"I don't see nothin'. Whatever you saw it didn't go across here," a voice said. "We would have seen it. No one could hide a horse out there among all them downed trees."

"Yeah. You're probably right. What caused all them trees to be knocked down?"

"Frank said a real strong wind just knocked them down. It happened several years ago."

"It looks kinda spooky ta me."

"Yeah. Let's get outa here."

Sam wasn't sure who the two talking were, but he knew they were either part of the Baker gang, or they at least knew Frank Baker.

"We best get on back. It was probably a deer or maybe an elk ya saw."

"Yeah. You're probably right. It's getting' on close to supper time, anyway."

Sam could hear the sounds of two men walking away. He stayed down just in case they had not gone.

After waiting for close to ten minutes, Sam took off his hat and slowly rose up to look over the fallen tree. He didn't see anyone, but he took a couple of minutes to scan the area just to be sure they had gone.

As soon as he thought it was safe, he stood up and nudged his horse to get him up. His horse stood up and shook itself. Sam slid his rifle into the scabbard, then swung himself up on the back of the horse. He rode his horse around the fallen trees and back into the forest.

It was getting late and Sam knew it would be getting dark soon. He began to look for a place where he could camp for the night. It had to be a place where he would not be found.

As Sam carefully rode through the woods, he worked his way away from the shale covered hillside and away from the trail. It was late when he found a rocky outcropping that would provide him with shelter, and where he would not be easily found. It would also provide him with a place where he could build a small fire to cook his meal of salt pork and coffee. He also had a couple of hard tack biscuits.

The rocky outcropping was high enough that his horse could walk under it without hitting his head on it. Sam took off his saddle, then hobbled his horse out a little ways from the overhanging rock so it could graze on the grass that grew nearby.

While his horse grazed, Sam built a small, almost smokeless, fire and fixed his dinner. When he was done eating, he laid out his bedroll. He leaned back and sipped on coffee while watching the fire burn out. He also spent sometime figuring out what he was going to do tomorrow. It occurred to him that he could go back across the open area of fallen trees and see if he could find the tracks of the two men that he had heard talking. If he could find them, there was a good chance they would lead him to Baker's hideout.

After the fire went out, Sam brought his horse in under the rocky overhang. He then laid down on his bedroll. He covered himself up, then listened to the sounds of the night. After awhile, he dosed off and slept.

* * * *

Sam was up with the first light of dawn. He got up and led his horse out to where there was some grass. As he stood next to his horse, he looked around. He thought the small meadow that stretched out before him was beautiful.

It seemed so peaceful and quiet, that was until he heard a bullet strike a small tree close to where he was standing. It was quickly followed by the sound of a rifle shot. Taking his horse in tow, Sam quickly ran into the woods where he would be out of sight. He ducked down behind some trees and looked out over the small meadow. He saw someone move in among the trees across the meadow near where the shot had come from. He had been seen. It was time to get out of there since he wasn't sure how many men were hunting him.

Sam quickly moved back to the shelter of the outcropping. He tossed his saddle on his horse along with his saddle bags and bedroll. Realizing that the outcropping would not be the safest place for him to holdup, he decided to take a shot at the one who shot at him, then quickly move off into the woods.

He found a place were he could rest his rifle for a long distant shot. Sam set his rifle over the rock and took careful aim at the only man he could see. It was obvious the man was being very careful, but not careful enough. He had unknowingly left himself exposed. Sam was sure that the man didn't know where Sam was because he was looking toward where he had been.

Sam slowly squeezed the trigger of his rifle. The rifle recoiled with a loud bang. Sam hit his mark. His bullet had struck the man in the upper left side of his chest, sending him over backwards.

Sam didn't wait to see if he had killed the man or not. It was time to get out of there before the rest of Baker's gang could come to the man's aid. He took the reins of his horse and moved off at a run to the end of the outcropping and quickly disappeared into the woods.

He had no more then disappeared into the woods when he heard several shots from across the meadow. He had seen the man fall and knew he had been hit hard. It was not likely that the man he had shot was able to fire back. There had to be someone else on the far side of the valley. He wondered if those shooting were the same two men he had encountered in the area where the trees had fallen. If it was, it wouldn't be long before the rest of the Baker gang would be out hunting for him. It was time to move out of the area.

Sam swung up in the saddle and began moving still deeper into the forest. He was positive he was not very far from where the gang had their hideout. He needed to find it. Once he did that, he would be able to plan his attack on the gang.

It wasn't long before Sam came across another trail. A quick look at the trail told him that it had been well used. He felt it was probably the main trail to the hideout.

Not wanting to expose himself any more than necessary, he turned and rode back into the woods just far enough that he could still see the trail between the trees. He then turned and slowly moved parallel to the trail.

As Sam moved along the trail, he stopped ever so often to listen. He had not heard a sound, but he felt that the wounded man would probably be brought along the trail. He didn't think they would leave him in the woods. They would want to take him somewhere to tend to his wounds, or to bury him if he had already died. He hadn't traveled very far when he heard the sound of horses. It was the dull sound of horse's hooves hitting the firm ground of the trail.

Sam quickly stepped out of the saddle and moved his horse behind some trees. He put one hand over the horse's nose to keep the horse quiet, while he drew his gun from his holster with the other. He could see the horses through the trees as they galloped along the trail.

The first horse had a rider on it. He was holding the reins of the second horse. There was a body slung over the saddle of the second horse. The man that Sam had shot had not lived long.

As Sam watched the two horses disappear down the trail, he was sure he had killed one of the gang members. He had reduced the gang by one, but he wasn't sure how many there might be. He knew of six from the reports he had received from those who had chased them into Hell's Canyon. That certainly didn't mean it was all of them. It was possible there were others who watched over the hideout whenever the rest of them went off to rob someone.

It was time to put a plan together on how he was going to get the rest of the gang. Since Sam had come up the mountain alone, there was no chance that help would be coming. If he went to get help, they might move their hideout somewhere else since it was obvious their hideout had been compromised. If they moved to someplace else, it could take months to find them again. With winter just around the corner, he didn't have time to try to find them again. He decided that his best and only chance of getting the gang was to eliminate them one at a time, if necessary.

Having served in the Union Army during the war, he had experience in "hit and run" type of fighting. It was not only effective when dealing with superior numbers, it caused confusion among the enemy. Confusion often caused the enemy to make mistakes.

Sam decided he would use his experience to get the gang. He would make them come after him, but he would not be in the same place twice.

He tied his horse to a tree back away from the trail, then took his rifle off his saddle. Being very careful not to be seen, he walked over to the trail and made a mark in the dirt that would help make it easier for him to find his horse in a hurry. He then walked off into the woods.

Sam worked his way alongside the trail that seemed to be well traveled. It wasn't long until he came to a place where he could see several log buildings. There were three people hanging around the rider and the horse with the body on it. But the ones that interested Sam the most were the three men who had just come out of one of the cabins.

They were all looking at the man who was slung over the saddle. It was clear that the three men were very angry. Sam recognized one of the men right away. He was Frank Baker, the leader of the gang.

Frank Baker was a fairly short man with broad shoulders, a barrel chest and a more than ample waist. He wore two pearl-handled six guns. He was known as a scrapper when it came to fighting. Frank was reported to be a fair hand with a gun, but preferred to fight with his fists. He had killed at least two men that Sam knew of with his bare hands.

Sam didn't know who the other two men were, but he was pretty sure the man who had brought the dead man in slung over the saddle was Slim Walker. Slim was known for his ability to handle a six shooter. Slim wore a single six shooter low on his right leg. He was not only fast, he was accurate with a gun. He was also quick to kill someone he didn't like, or who had made him mad. Sam recalled that it didn't seem to take much to make him mad.

It was time to start his "hit and run" attack on the Baker gang. He wanted to take Baker out of the mix as soon as possible. He was the leader. His death might cause confusion among the others, but there was a problem. There was a horse standing between him and Sam, which made the shot difficult and chancy. Sam decided to pick another target. His choice of a target would be Slim because he was the one who was the most dangerous in a gunfight.

Sam put his rifle barrel in the crook of a tree and took careful aim at Slim. He slowly pulled the trigger. The gun fired just as Slim moved. Sam's shot missed Slim by inches, but hit one of the other men who had been behind Slim out of Sam's sight.

Sam quickly turned and began running through the woods to his horse. He didn't wait to see if he had killed the other man. As he ran, he could hear gunfire. He was sure they would be coming after him very quickly.

Once he got to his horse, he swung up in the saddle and wasted no time in riding away. Sam headed across the trail and began working his way further north into a very rocky area. He knew it was the one place where he could hideout and plan his next move. It was also a place where he could move around with little chance of being seen. It was a good place to carry out a "hit and run" attack if they decided to chase him into the rocks. If they came after him, which he was sure they would, Sam would be able to shoot and move almost undetected.

Under the circumstance, Sam had made no effort to cover his tracks. In fact, he wanted them to follow him. Once he was in the rocks, Sam picked a place where he could see anyone who might come out of the cover of the woods while following his trail. The first one out in the open was the one most likely to die first.

Sam sat on a rock behind a bolder and listened for any sound that might be made by a man or horse. Keeping undercover as much as possible, Sam watched and waited. He began to think they might not come out into the open. If they thought he was hiding in the rocks, they might spread out and circle around in the hope of trapping him in among the rocks.

Sam was beginning to think he might have made a mistake moving into the rocks. He quickly took the reins of his horse and began to walk him among the rocks. He moved at a ninety degree angle from where he had come into the rocks.

Once he had his horse back into the woods, he found a place near the edge of the woods where he could hide both himself and his horse. It gave him a good view of the open rocky area while still having good cover and a good escape route should things get a little too hot to hang around. Sam hid in a cluster of bushes and waited.

It seemed to take a long time before anyone showed up. Sam saw a man approach the edge of the woods. The man was being very cautious as he looked out into the rocks. It was obvious that the man had been following Sam's tracks.

Sam watched the man very carefully hoping that whoever might be with him would show themselves. Placing his rifle over a tree branch that had fallen over the bolder he was hiding behind, Sam put his sights on the man. He watched the man's movements while still glancing around in the hope of seeing if there was anyone else.

It wasn't long before he saw another man look out from behind a tree at the edge of the woods. The second man was about twenty feet to the left of the first man. They were both being very cautious. Staying close behind the trees, neither of the two men offered Sam much of a target.

Suddenly, both men looked toward the wooded area off to Sam's right. Sam wasn't sure if there was another of the men working his way around the edge of the woods, or if there had been something else that had caught their attention. Not knowing what was there, Sam pulled back deeper into the woods. He took hold of the reins to his horse, then quietly retreated away from the area.

Sam made a wide circle around to his right. Holding the reins of his horse in one hand, he worked his way around behind where he had seen the men. He thought if he could get behind them, he might be able to get closer to their camp while they were away from it. He might be able to find a place where he could watch them without anyone seeing him. Knowing what they were doing would give him the advantage.

It took Sam the better part of an hour to work his way around behind the two men he had seen at the edge of the woods. He found their horses and where they had been tied before he found the men. They were still being very cautious, but had apparently not seen any movement across the open rocky area. The first one to step out into the rocky area moved slowly between some of the larger rocks. When he did move, he moved crouched over to make himself as small a target as possible, but it wasn't small enough.

Sam could see him clearly as he moved slowly out among the rocks. Sam laid his rifle across a tree branch and took careful aim. He slowly pulled the trigger. His shot caught the man in his side causing him to fall over.

It was time for Sam to get out of there, and he wasted no time in doing it. He knew his shot had hit the man hard. He didn't wait to see if he had killed the man, but he knew that the man would be out of action.

The other man in the rocks quickly ducked down. He didn't return fire as he could not see where the shot had come from. He was playing it very cautiously. He had no desire to give Sam a chance to shoot him.

There was one more down. That left at least four of the robbers. How many others lived in the little gathering of buildings, Sam didn't know. He also didn't know if the others would take sides, and if they did which side they would take.

The sun was beginning to set and it would be dark before long. It was time for Sam to find a place to hide for the night. As he moved through the darkening forest, he began to think that it might be a good idea if he could find a place near the buildings. He might be able to get another one of the gang in the dark.

As he moved through the woods, he circled around so that he was on the opposite side of the buildings. He found a place to hobble his horse that was far enough from the buildings so they would not be able to hear it.

Sam slowly moved closer to the buildings. When he was close enough he could hear them talking, he settled in to listen.

"Anyone know who that shooter is," Baker said.

"No. He's been shootin' then runnin'. It's almost as if'n there's more 'n one out there."

"We best keep a watch." Slim said. "Billy, you go out and keep watch."

Sam watched the front of the cabin. When Billy came out, he had his rifle aimed right at the kids chest. He noticed Billy moved over to a dark corner of the cabin's porch and leaned against the wall. It made it much harder for Sam to see him.

Sam watched Billy for several minutes. The sun had set and it was getting dark. The only light was the light that came out through the open door and the one window in front. It gave Sam an idea.

Sam pulled back then circled around behind the cabin. He silently moved up alongside the cabin to the corner. Being very careful, he held a pistol in his hand as he slowly turned the corner. He stuck the barrel of his gun against Billy's head. Billy froze.

"One wrong move and you will die," Sam whispered. "Very slowly give me your gun."

Billy cooperated without a sound. Sam motioned for him to step around the corner. He then laid the end of his pistol over the back of Billy's head, knocking him to the ground unconscious. Sam then moved over next to the window and peered inside.

Baker was sitting at the table facing the door. Slim was also at the table. He was sitting with his side to the door. There was one other man sitting at the table, but Sam didn't know who he was or anything about him. Yet, it was clear he was a member of the gang.

It was time to take action or pull out. Three of the members of the gang were either dead, shot up, or lying out cold on the ground. Sam decided it was time to end this. Putting a gun in each hand, Sam stepped in front of the open door.

"Don't do anything stupid," Sam said as he pointed his guns at the men at the table.

He had caught the rest of the gang off guard. They just looked at him as if he was crazy, which was just about how Sam was feeling at the moment. He had forgotten for the moment about those who lived there, but it was too late now.

All of a sudden, the three men at the table started to move at once. It happened so quickly that Sam reacted without conscious thought as he fired three shots. His first shot caught Slim square in the chest with his hand on his gun. His second shot caught Baker in the right shoulder dumping him back over the chair he had been sitting on, while his third shot went wide of the third man. However, he was able to get off a fourth shot at the third man, but not before he took a bullet to his left arm. Sam's fourth shot had hit the man in his gut.

When the smoke cleared, there were three outlaws lying on the floor. Slim had died on the floor, Baker was still alive, but was bleeding badly from the shot to his shoulder. The third man was laying on the floor gut-shot and in a great deal of pain.

Just then, Sam heard footsteps running toward the cabin. He leaned against the wall near the door. Two young women and an old man came running into the building. They stopped when they saw the three outlaws. One of the young women turned around and saw Sam leaning against the wall. He was holding his gun on them.

"You are hurt," the young woman said. "We must help you."

Sam wasn't sure what he should do. He was feeling very weak. It was becoming hard for him to think clearly just before he passed out.

* * * *

When Sam woke, he found himself in a bed. His left arm was hurting. He turned his head and looked around the room. His gun and gun belt were hanging over a chair only a few feet from the bed. His marshal's badge was hooked to the belt. He heard a noise and turned his head the other way and saw a young woman cooking something on the stove. She turned, looked at him and smiled.

"Good morning," she said. "How are you feeling?"

"Alive."

"That is good. Are you hungry?"

"Yes."

He watched her as she dished up what looked like soup of some kind into a bowl. She walked toward him, then set the soup on a table. She leaned over him and arranged his pillows so he could sit up. She sat down on a stool next to the bed and began to feed him.

"We found your horse in the woods. We are taking very good care of it."

"What about Baker and his men? What happened to them?"

"We buried three of them this morning. Billy, the one you hit on the head, is locked in the ice house."

"What about the one I shot in the woods," Sam asked.

"We found him, too. We buried him in the woods. We have been their prisoners for a very long time. We are glad that you came to free us," the young woman said with a smile.

Sam didn't say anything. He stayed there until he was able to ride. He bid his goodbyes and took his one prisoner back to Hill City. He turned him over to the sheriff, and told his story to the sheriff before he moved on.

STAGECOACH TO NOWHERE

It was late in the morning when the stagecoach arrived in Faith for a change of horses. Once the horses were changed, it would head on to the next stage station. There were three passengers who got off the stagecoach.

The first passenger was a tall, lean young man. He was wearing a well-worn cowboy hat, a plaid shirt and jeans. His chaps looked like they had seen a lot of use, and his boots had seen better days. He had a Colt .45 strapped to his waist and a Winchester '73 he held loosely in one hand.

The second passenger was a slim young woman who was dressed in a red dress with a long full skirt that had several petticoats under it. The waist was narrow showing off her fine figure. She wore a matching bonnet with curls of long dark hair hanging down from under it.

The last passenger was a short little man who was wearing a suit that had frayed cuffs. The collar of his shirt was a bit ragged, too.

The spats he wore were yellowed by the dust and dirt. He had the look of a man who was rather tired and unhappy.

The three passengers had gotten out of the stagecoach to stretch their legs. As soon as the horses were changed for fresh ones, the stagecoach was ready to continue its trip west. The three passengers got back in the stagecoach.

As soon as the passengers were seated, the driver yelled at the team of horses and the stagecoach lunged forward. The stagecoach rocked back and forth until the horses pulling the coach settled into a steady pace. It was only a matter of minutes before the stagecoach was well on its way.

There was a slight wind out of the northwest that kept most of the dust kicked up by the horses and stagecoach from drifting inside. The passengers settled in for the long rather rough ride. The young woman looked at the cowboy. He looked like he might know the route they were taking.

"Excuse me, sir. Do you know where we will be stopping next?" the young woman asked.

"My name is Clint Foster, and yes, Ma'am. It's Nowhere."

"Nowhere?" she asked as she looked into his eyes to see if he was telling her the truth.

"Yes, Ma'am. It's called that because someone said it was in the middle of nowhere."

"Is there anything near it?"

"No, Ma'am, not yet. It's just a stage stop for fresh horses. You can get a little something to eat there if you're hungry. I get off the stage there."

"Excuse me for prying into your affairs, Mr. Foster, but why are you getting off if there is nothing there?"

"Please, call me Clint. Mr. Foster makes me feel old," he said with a grin.

"All right," the young woman said with a slight grin. "I'm Mary Spencer."

"Nice to meet you, Miss Spencer."

"Mary, please."

"Okay, Mary."

"Why did you say, 'not yet'?"

"Because I'm going to start my ranch there."

"How are you going to start a ranch without any horses?" she said with a slight grin.

"I sent a string of horses and supplies on ahead. They should be in the corral at Nowhere stage station by the time we get there."

"Oh," she replied as she looked at him wondering if he was being truthful.

"I worked for the stage line a few months ago when they were having trouble with some Indians. They agreed to send my horses and supplies on ahead with their supplies for the station."

"I see," Mary replied.

She thought that Clint was smart to do that. It would save him a lot of work and a lot of time in the saddle. Although the stagecoach was not very comfortable, it was still more comfortable than being in the saddle all day, day after day.

"How far are you goin'?" Clint asked.

"I'm planning on going as far as Fort Meade," she said, not really wanting to tell him any more.

"Do you have a soldier waiting for you there?"

"Yes. Well, not really," she said as she looked down at her hands folded in her lap.

Clint looked at her for a moment then turned and looked out the window. Since she didn't answer him, he thought that she might feel it was none of his business.

Mary wondered if she should tell him more about her trip to Fort Meade. She was on her way to visit her brother who was stationed at the fort. She was going there because their parents had died, and she had no reason to stay in the east. She had no money and no job to support herself. She was hoping she could find work in the town near the fort where her brother was stationed.

She leaned back, closed her eyes and let her mind wonder. Her thoughts turned to Clint. He seemed to be polite and had dreams of a future. She wondered what it would be like to have such lofty dreams, and be willing to work hard to make them come true. She couldn't help but admire him for it.

It occurred to her that he was probably as broke as she was. She had little more to her name, than the clothes in her chest and those on her back. She barely had enough money to get to Fort Meade. Mary was sure Clint would be as broke as she was once he bought his cattle. But then, he would still have the cattle and his dream. She suddenly realized that she didn't even have a dream.

Mary's thoughts were disturbed by Clint waking her. She had not realized that she had fallen asleep. She looked at him. She was confused by the sound of his voice.

"Mary, get down," he said. "Get down on the floor."

Still looking at him, she hesitated, but only for a second. Everything became very real with the sound of rifle shots. She quickly slid down on the floor of the coach, while Clint turned his attention to outside the coach. Clint stuck his rifle out the window and began shooting.

The stagecoach was under attack by fifteen Indians. The driver was pushing the stage as fast as the horses could run. They still had a long way to go to get to the next stage station. There was little chance that they would be able to get there before the Indians would be upon them.

The little man was quickly awakened by the commotion, and drew the small gun he carried under his coat. He began to give return fire on the Indians, but he didn't look like he was aiming at anything when he fired. He just fired his gun out the window without aiming it.

There was shooting coming from on top of the stagecoach as well. It sounded as if Max, the man riding shotgun, was putting up a good fight from the top of the stagecoach. By the sounds of it, he was using a rifle.

The rapid firing from the stagecoach discouraged the Indians and they pulled back. At first, it looked like they might have given up on the attack.

There were some sighs of relief until Clint began to realize what the Indians were really doing. They had not pulled back. Instead, they were swinging out in a wide circle to the north staying well away from the stagecoach and out of range of the guns Clint and the others had. Clint had seen this done before. They were going to swing wide around in an effort to get in front of stagecoach where they could shoot the horses.

Clint looked around. The Indians had chosen to swing wide around to the north side of the coach where the land was flat and they would be able to keep an eye on the stagecoach. Clint noticed there was a wash with a high cliff behind it just to the south. He swung out the side of the coach and yelled up at the driver to head for the wash.

Fred, the driver, was unable to hear what Clint had said, but he looked to where Clint was pointing. He nodded his head, then started the horses toward the wash. When he got to the wash, he saw a place where the stagecoach could be driven down into it. He turned the horses into the wash then drew them up to a stop.

Clint and Max got out of the stagecoach and took positions on the edge of the wash to protect the stagecoach, while Fred unharnessed the horses. Fred tied the horses to the side of the stagecoach closest to the cliff. It put the horses between the cliff and the stagecoach to better protect them from gunfire from the Indians.

Clint watched the Indians for awhile before he pulled back from the edge of the wash. He walked back behind the stagecoach to talk to Fred.

"What do you think?" Fred asked Clint.

"I think we stand a better chance here than in the open."

"I agree, but if it comes to a long fight we could find ourselves a little short of bullets."

"I've got some bullets in my stuff, but not enough for a long fight."

"Well, it might be enough to hold them off until dark or until we can get some help," Fred said.

"There's not much cover for them out there. We'll need to watch for them to try to come up the wash to get at us. They ain't likely to attack us straight on with no cover."

"How about putting a man on the top of the stagecoach? He might be able to see what's going on with them Indians before they try something," Fred said.

"Good idea."

Fred motioned for Max to climb up on the stagecoach and keep an eye out. Clint took his rifle and moved over to the edge of the wash and watched the Indians.

The Indians had never had a stagecoach take cover in the wash and setup a defense so quickly. Most of the time, the stagecoach would try to outrun the Indians while shooting at them. It was difficult to hit anything when shooting from a moving stagecoach, but a stopped stagecoach was different.

The Indians were a little confused by the sudden change in strategy. They sat on their horses some distance away from where the stagecoach had come to a stop. The Indians were sure they were well out of range. They had gathered close together to discuss how they would attack the stagecoach with the least danger to themselves.

Clint laid over the edge of the wash and watched the Indians. He was sure they were trying to figure out how to continue their attack. As they gathered together to talk, Clint had an idea. If it worked it could end the standoff.

Clint drew his rifle up to his shoulder and took careful aim. He then raised the end of his rifle a little and slowly pulled the trigger. The loud bang of his Winchester startled everyone near the coach. The Indians didn't hear it until after one of the braves fell from his horse with a bullet hole in his chest.

The startled Indians were surprised that they had been attacked when they were so far away from the coach. They didn't know what to think and milled around in a confused state.

Clint fired a second shot before the Indians could figure out what was happening. It wasn't until the second shot from near the stagecoach hit another brave that they began to understand. The bullet passed through the Indian's leg and hit his horse sending both of them to the ground. The rest of the Indians quickly rode further away from the stagecoach and those shooting at them.

Everyone at the coach was looking at Clint. They had a hard time believing that he had actually shot two Indians at such a long distance.

"I'll be darned. I ain't never seen shootin' like that," Fred said with a grin. "How'd you do that?"

"Just a little Kentucky windage," Clint said with a grin. "I learned how to do that from my dad. He was a sharpshooter during the war."

"It looks like they've decided to leave," Max called from on top of the stagecoach.

"We best be getting out of here 'for they change their minds," Fred said.

The men hitched up the stagecoach, then everyone got aboard. Fred drove the stagecoach out of the wash and they started on toward Nowhere at a run.

They were not on the road for very long when Mary looked over at Clint and smiled. Clint smiled back.

"You know that you saved all our lives?"

"Yes, Ma'am. I know, but you've got to remember I was saving my own hide as well," he said with a big grin.

"Did you see what the little man was doing while you and the others were defending the stagecoach?" she whispered.

"No. I was a little busy."

"He was cowering and shooting without looking where he was shooting."

"Well, I wouldn't be too hard on him. None of us want to die."

"But he was being a coward."

"Maybe, but how are any of us to know how we will react when faced with the strong likelihood of losing our life."

Mary turned and looked at the little man. He was looking back at her. She wondered what he was thinking. She was also thinking about what Clint had said. She began to think about herself. What would I have done if I had had a gun, she wondered.

"I would like to thank you for running those Indians off," Mary said as she turned and looked at Clint.

"You're welcome," Clint said as he looked at her.

"What would you have done if your shooting at them had not worked?"

"I would have given you a gun and told you to shoot back. I would have also told you to, - - ah - -, well that's what I would have told you," Clint said then looked away.

"What would you have also told me?"

"It ain't important now. They're gone."

Mary looked into his eyes. He was not telling her something that she should know, she was sure of it. She sat there and continued to look at him while she was trying to think of what it was he was not saying. He was looking at the floor of the stagecoach. Then it came to her.

"I think what you would have told me was to save the last cartridge for myself. Isn't that right?"

Clint didn't look at her. She was right and he knew it. He didn't want to tell a lady that if all was lost she should shoot herself.

"Isn't that right?" she asked him again as she reached out and put her hand on his hand.

He slowly turned and looked at her. Clint didn't say anything. As he thought about the woman sitting next to him, he began to understand that she had a lot more sand than just about any woman he had known. Clint began to realize she was not only beautiful, she was a strong woman.

"Yes, Ma'am," he said softly. "I would not want them Indians to get hold of you. They do some terrible things to white people they catch, especially women."

"I understand. I have been told of such things," she said.

Mary gently squeezed his hand. She looked up at him for a moment, then turned and looked out the side window. However, she did not let go of his hand.

Clint did not try to take his hand from hers, either. Instead, he let her hold his hand. It felt good, and he certainly didn't mind having a pretty young woman hold his hand.

* * * *

The rest of the trip to Nowhere was without incident. They arrived pretty much on schedule. The passengers got out of the stagecoach while Fred and Max unharnessed the horses and led them to the corral.

They had no more than put the horses in the corral when a shot was fired that struck the edge of the door to the station. Clint dropped his saddle then swung around clutching his rifle in both hands. He saw the first of several Indians riding hard toward the station. He raised his rifle to his shoulder and pulled the trigger. The Indian closest to him was hit square in the chest and fell to the ground. Without thinking, he swung around to shoot at another Indian and hit that one as well. With two of the Indians already down, the rest made a hasty retreat for cover in a narrow ravine not very far from the front of the station.

Fred and Max scrambled toward the station. The driver made it inside with the rest of the passengers, but Max took a bullet in the leg. He fell in the dirt outside the stage station.

"Cover me," Clint yelled as he ran out to get Max.

While Clint grabbed Max, he could hear the sounds of rifle and pistol fire. Several bullets hit near him as he picked up Max and ran toward the station.

As he ran into the station, he heard the heavy wooden door slam shut behind him. He put Max on a bed, then went to a window while the woman at the station and Mary looked after Max.

It was clear that the Indians were hoping to get as many of those at the station as possible before they could get to cover. It was also obvious to Clint and Fred they were there to steal the horses. Clint could not let it happen as several of the horses in the corral were his. He was going to need them to start his ranch. Without them, he would have to go to work for someone else to make enough money to buy a new string of horses.

"We have to keep them away from the horses," Clint said as he opened the shutters on one of the windows. "If they get the horses, they will have us trapped here."

Clint could see an Indian creeping toward the corral. He took careful aim and slowly pulled the trigger. His gun went off. He saw the Indian double over in pain. He had hit the Indian, but was not sure it had put him out of the fight completely.

The sudden sound of shots being fired on the other side of the window caused him to turn and look. He saw Mary at the window with a gun in her hand.

"Are you all right, Mary?" Clint asked.

Mary turned and looked at him. The look on her face was one he had seen on a good many young men after they had shot and killed their first man.

"I'm fine," she said with little conviction in her voice. "You need to watch the corral."

Clint smiled at her then turned back to the window. He was proud of her. She had stood her ground and was helping to defend the station.

Suddenly a bullet slammed against the window frame where Clint was watching. It splattered small fragments of wood in his face. One of the pieces of wood cut his cheek, but there was no time to worry about a minor wound.

Clint again found a target and fired. He didn't waste a single shot. He made them count as ammunition was in short supply.

Suddenly there were shots being fired from all sides of the station, both inside and out. It was followed by the sound of a bugle, an Army bugle.

Clint could see U.S. Army Calvary troops charging toward the stage station. It was clear they had heard the shooting and had seen what was going on.

The officer leading the troops motioned for his men to continue to chase the Indians while he stopped in front of the station. The young officer dismounted just as Clint stepped outside to greet him.

"You're sure a welcome sight."

"Glad we got here in time. I'm Lieutenant John Spencer with the fifth Calvary unit out of Fort Meade."

"Nice to meet you, Lieutenant. I think there's someone inside who you would like to meet."

"Oh, really," he said looking at Clint as if he was not sure what he meant.

Lieutenant Spencer went inside the station. As soon as he saw Mary, he began to grin. He had not expected to see her there. Mary did not notice him at first because she was helping to care for Max.

"Mary," John said.

Mary turned at the sound of his voice. She smiled when she recognized him then ran to him. She put her arms around his neck and hugged her brother.

Clint stood back and watched the reunion with a smile. Mary turned and looked at Clint.

"Clint, this is my brother John."

"We met," Clint said. "You should be proud of your sister. She's a fighter."

"She always has been. She's also strong headed," John said with a smile.

"Now that's not fair. I'm just determined to get what I want," Mary said.

Mary and John went off in a corner to talk. Clint went outside to give them a chance to talk in private.

While Clint was outside, the troopers returned. Clint stopped the Sergeant from going inside. At first the Sergeant wasn't going to listen to Clint, but changed his mind when he was told that Lieutenant Spencer was talking with his sister from back east.

After a while, John and Mary came out of the stage station. John walked over to Clint.

"Mary told me what you did out there. That must have been a sight to see. I'll bet the Indians were surprised."

"I think they were," Clint said with a grin. "

"Well, I'm sure glad that you were on the stagecoach," John said.

"I was just trying to stay alive."

"Thanks, anyway. We're going to spend the night here, then we will escort the stagecoach to the next stop."

"I hope you have a safe trip to the fort, but this is where I get off."

"Here? There's nothing out here," John said as he looked around.

"There's nothing here now, but there will be. I'm going to start a ranch. Those extra horses in the corral are mine.

"I take it you plan to build a home out here?" John asked.

"That, and a corral. I'll have to build a barn of sorts to winter the horses in, but I'll manage."

"It sounds like you've got things planned out pretty well."

"I do. I have the place picked out for a barn and a house. Now if I can get the Indians to leave me alone, I'll do just fine."

"Well, good luck with that. I'll try to stop by when we are out this way on patrol," John said.

"You'd be welcome. My place will be about three miles straight north of here."

"Again thanks for looking after Mary."

"Glad to do it," Clint said then walked over to the corral to take care of his horses.

* * * *

The next morning, Clint stood by the front door of the stage station. When Mary came out, he spoke to her.

"Can I call on you sometime?"

"I would like that. I would like to know how you are doing. I think it's wonderful that you have a dream and the courage to make it come true," she said.

"I'll be in touch," Clint promised.

Mary smiled at him, then walked over to the stagecoach. She looked back at him for a second, then got in. She sat next to a window and watched him as the coach pulled away. She wondered if he would keep in touch with her. The coach headed off along the trail followed by Lieutenant John Spencer and his men.

Clint watched the coach for a little while, then went to the corral to get his horses. As soon as he was ready, he headed straight north of the stage station to a place he had picked out almost two years ago. There was a narrow river that flowed through a shallow valley. The grass was green and thick in the valley, and there were cottonwood trees on both sides of the river for as far as he could see. It was the prettiest place he had ever seen.

Clint went right to work making himself a shelter among the cottonwoods close to the river. It would be his home until he could get a sod house built. He cut wood from the cottonwood trees for his house. He planned to build it part way up the side of the hill on the east side of the river. It would overlook the stream that flowed by only about fifty yards away, and he would be able to watch the sunset from the front door at the end of the day. After cutting into the side of the hill and building the walls, he cut large timbers to make a roof. He then cut large squares of sod thick with grass and laid them neatly and tightly together over large logs for a roof. When he was finished with the house, he had a strong good sized home. With the stone fireplace he built to cook in and to keep it warm, it was very comfortable. The sod house would be cool in the summer and easy to keep warm in the winter. It was hard work, but the extra horses made hauling logs much easier.

During his first year, he also built a sod barn in the side of hill. He built it in such a way that two sides were made by cutting into the hill side. The other two sides were made of logs. He then built a corral that was larger than he really needed out in front of it. He was planning ahead.

One other thing he did during the first year was to write to Mary and tell her about how his ranch was coming along. He would take his letter to the stage station at Nowhere when he went for supplies. He would leave his letter to be taken to Fort Meade on the next stagecoach going west. He told her about everything he had done to get it ready to live there. The nice thing about it was, she wrote back to him. In one letter she had told him that she was looking forward to seeing his ranch.

By late the next Spring, he had his place ready to start his ranch. He was now ready to get some cattle and start ranching. All his work with cattle would be for him, not for someone else. It was his ranch and he would not have to take orders from anyone.

Clint knew of a place near Belle Fourche where he could get some cattle. It was time to go get them. It was also time for him to stop at Fort Meade and talk to Mary. He had a very important question to ask her.

Clint left for Belle Fourche with a string of horse. It took him several days to get to Fort Meade. It was one of the places he wanted to stop. All the time he had been building up his ranch, he had thought of no one but Mary Spencer. He planned to ask her to marry him, but was nervous about what she would say. She was such a fine looking woman, and well educated. He was worried that she might not want to live in a sod house. It was not the house he planned to have in the future. He knew there was only one way for him to find out if she would marry him, and that was to ask her.

He arrived at the fort in the late afternoon. He tied his string of horse in a grassy place just outside the fort, then walked toward the commanding officer's office. He was greeted by a young man standing guard at the door.

"May I help you, sir," the young soldier asked.

"I would like to see Lieutenant John Spencer, if he's around."

"If you'll wait here, I'll see if he's around. What's your name, sir?"

"Clint Foster."

The young soldier turned and stepped inside the building. Clint stood on the porch of the building and looked around while he waited. He could see several soldiers posted around the fort, and a couple of them over near a long building that looked like it could house a good number of soldiers. They looked like they were washing clothes. He heard the door open behind him and turned around.

"Clint, it is good to see you. What brings you here? Are you having problems out there?" John asked showing his concern.

"No problems. I have a few Indians come by and watch me work from time to time, but no trouble from them. I came by to see Mary."

"She's over at my house. It's the one across the parade grounds," John said as he pointed to a small house across an open area. "I'll go with you."

John stepped off the porch and started across the parade grounds. Clint quickly joined him and walked beside him.

"She has been keeping me posted on your progress with your ranch. It sounds like you are about ready to get some livestock."

Clint didn't know what to say, but he was glad to hear that she seemed interested in what he was building out on the prairie. He could only hope she would be glad to see him.

"I am. I'm on my way to Belle Fourche to get some breeding stock"

As they got closer to John's quarters, Clint began to wonder if he should have written her and told her he was coming to see her. She might not like him dropping in on her.

"John, do you think she will mind that I didn't tell her I was coming?"

"I think she will be very glad to see you," he said with a grin.

John stepped up on the porch and opened the door.

"Mary, we have company."

Mary came out of a room off to the side. Her eyes got big and her jaw dropped when she saw Clint. A smile came over her face and she hurried across the room to greet him. She threw her arms around him and hugged him.

Clint didn't know what to do, but he knew enough to wrap her in his arms and hug her. She leaned back and looked up at him. She wasn't sure why he was there, but she was glad he was. She finally stepped back and looked up at him.

"What brings you here? Is everything all right at the ranch?"

"Yes and no," he said as he took a deep breath.

"I don't understand," she said with a confused look on her face.

"The ranch is not a ranch, yet, but I hope it will be soon."

"I still don't understand. What will it take to make it the ranch you have dreamed about?" she asked.

"It will take some cattle, breeding stock mostly to begin with," he said, then took another deep breath. "And it will take – a – a woman to make it the ranch I have always dreamed of."

Mary looked at him. She wasn't sure what he was saying.

"I came by to see if you – ah – might – ah – be - - -."

"Yes. Yes," she said with excitement. "I would love to be the woman to share your dream."

Clint grinned from ear to ear as she threw her arms around his neck and kissed him.

"Would I be out of line if I said it looks like we are going to have a wedding here at the fort?" John said with a grin.

Mary looked up at Clint as if waiting for Clint to say something.

"That depends on Mary," Clint said then turned to look at Mary. "Will you marry me?"

"Yes, I will marry you," she said then looked at her brother. "And, yes, there is going to be a wedding at the fort."

"I'm going to Belle Fourche for cattle when I leave here." Clint said. "I thought I would get the cattle and take them to the ranch, then come back and marry you here."

"Why don't we get married while you are here?" Mary asked. "We can have the Post Chaplin marry us, then I will go with you to get the cattle. I don't know much about herding cattle, but I can learn. I want to be a part of your dream."

Clint didn't know what to say. He had not expected her to be so willing to help him take the cattle back to the ranch. He had already hired several men to help him with the herd. "You might as well give in," John said with a grin. "I'll make the arrangements. You can have your wedding in the morning, then leave for Belle Fourche.

John left the house so that Clint and Mary could talk. What Mary had said made a lot of sense. It would save a lot of time and travel. The trip to Belle Fourche and a night in a hotel could be looked at as their honeymoon. It wasn't much of a honeymoon, but it was more than most frontier women had gotten.

Clint set up camp just outside the fort. He spent as much time with Mary as he could. They had a lot to talk about.

The next morning, Clint and Mary were married with John as best man and the colonel's wife as the bridesmaid. After the wedding, there was a small reception before the newlyweds were sent off on their new adventure.

Mr. and Mrs. Clint Foster got the cattle they needed to start their ranch. When they arrived back at the ranch with the cattle, Mary suggested they hang a sign over the front gate that read "Somewhere".

Over the years, their ranch grew. They eventually raised large herds of cattle and hired several men to help on the ranch. They also had six children, four boys and two girls.

THE TEACHER AND
THE SHOOTIST

Miss Anna Bateman, the local school teacher, was enjoying a pleasant walk down the main street of the small mining town of Deadwood. She had just left the Saturday morning Bible study at the church. She was walking to the Mercantile Store to get a few things.

As she approached some of the local miners, they moved out of her way and tipped their hats to her. She smiled politely, but continued to walk on by without saying a word. She was well known in town, and was thought well of by most of the community.

Anna was a very lovely young woman, and there was no shortage of suitors in her life. There wasn't a single young man in the area that hadn't tried to call on her, but she had refused them all. She seemed like a rather shy young woman, and made it a point to stay away from the men. She even went so far as to look away when a man looked at her, but things were about to change.

A surly looking buckskin horse came walking down the street toward her. The horse looked like it had traveled a long ways and wasn't about to take any guff from anyone.

On the horse's back was a tall, lean young man. He was wearing a buckskin shirt and trousers. His pants were tucked in his high-topped moccasins with a knife sticking out the top of the right one. He had a wide brimmed hat that put most of his face in the shadow of the brim, making it hard for anyone to see his eyes. He had a gun on his hip that looked like it had been well used.

The rider eased the horse over next to the boardwalk. The horse's head was leaning over the boardwalk in front of Anna, forcing her to stop if she didn't want to step off the boardwalk into the dirt.

Anna had not noticed the young man until his horse stood in her way. She stepped back away from the horse and looked up at the rider. Her first thought was to tell him to move his horse out of her way, but didn't say anything as she looked at the rider.

"Sorry about my horse, Ma'am, but he just can't help but stop when there's a pretty girl around," the rider said with a pleasant smile.

"My name's John," he said as he looped one leg over the saddle horn, then reached up and tipped his hat back. "John Tucker."

Anna just stood there and looked at him. She couldn't help but notice that he was very handsome in a rugged sort of way. He had a very pleasant smile, and sparkling blue eyes. He also had broad shoulders. She found it hard not to look at him.

"I didn't get your name, Ma'am."

"Ah – I'm – ah. Would you please get your horse out of my way," she finally said.

"Now is that anyway to be. He just wants to say, hi."

"Well, I think he has said, hi. Now may I go on my way?"

"Yes, Ma'am," he said.

John swung his leg back over the saddle, then gently pulled the reins back. His horse backed up a couple of steps to allow Anna to pass. As she walked by, she glanced up at John, but didn't say anything as he reached up and touched the brim of his hat.

John continued to watch her as she walked on down the boardwalk. It wasn't until she turned down a side street that he looked down at his horse.

"She is a pretty girl, don't you think?" he said to his horse, but his horse didn't respond.

John turned his horse and started down the street toward the Sheriff's Office. He stopped in front of the Sheriff's Office and swung down from the saddle. He looked around as he tied his horse to the hitching rail. He didn't see anyone who might cause him a problem. He turned around and walked into the Sheriff's Office.

The sheriff was sitting in a chair with his feet on the desk. He glanced up at John and gave him the once over. It was clear to the sheriff that this young man was a dangerous man. The sheriff swung his feet off the desk and sat up.

"Somethin' I can do for ya?" the sheriff asked.

"I'm looking for a man by the name of Jack Storm. In Indian country, he's known as Indian Jack."

"What do you want with him?"

"He's wanted for murdering a storekeeper in cold blood over by Yankton on the Missouri River," John said as he took a wanted poster out of his shirt pocket.

He handed the wanted poster to the sheriff and watched him while he looked at it. John wasn't sure what was going through the sheriff's mind, but he seemed to be studying the poster very closely.

The sheriff turned and looked up at John and said, "He may be wanted over that way, but he ain't wanted here."

"That's a wanted dead or alive poster. I intend to take him alive, if I can."

"I doubt that you could take him either way, young man. You're mighty young to be a bounty hunter," the sheriff said with a slight grin.

It was clear what the sheriff had said didn't set well with John. Hunting for Indian Jack was not the first man that he had hunted down.

"I'm not one bit interested in what you think I can do or can't do. I'm looking for Indian Jack and I intend to find him. All I want to know is have you seen him around here?"

"Yeah, I've seen him, but you better understand me. If you shoot him down in the street, I'll be hanging you the next day. He ain't done nothin' wrong here."

John just looked at the sheriff. He wasn't sure why the sheriff was so set on protecting a killer. He couldn't help but think that the sheriff was afraid of Indian Jack.

"I've got just one thing to say to you, Sheriff. It would be best if you just stay out of my way."

Without further comment, John turned around and started out the door. He didn't even give the sheriff time to respond to his last comment.

John stood in front of the Sheriff's Office and looked up and down the street. He was trying to figure out where he might find Indian Jack. It was early in the day. The more he thought about it, the more he was sure that

Indian Jack was very likely sleeping off a drunk. He knew Jack liked to drink and was known to be a mean drunk. Most of the people he had killed, he had killed while drunk.

Just as he was about to untie his horse from the hitching rail, he saw the pretty young woman he had met when he first arrived in Deadwood. He realized she had never told him what her name was, but he would correct that. He watched her as she walked along the boardwalk. She was carrying a grocery sack.

He turned and was about to mount his horse when he heard some rather loud voices. One of them was a woman's voice. John turned to see a big burly man reach out and grab Anna by the arm causing her to drop the sack of groceries. He dropped the reins of his horse and hurried across the street.

"Whoa there," John said as he stepped up behind the big man. "I don't think the young lady wishes to go with you."

The big man turned and looked at John, then said. "Mind your own business."

John didn't say anything. He could see the fear in Anna's eyes. It was as if she was pleading with him to help her.

"I think you should let the lady go," John said in a causal way.

"Get lost little fella. This ain't none of your business," he said just as Anna tried to jerk herself free.

The big guy turned and looked at Anna. It was a big mistake to look away from John. When he did, John swiftly drew his gun and laid the barrel over the back of the big man's head. The big man let go of Anna and went crashing to the ground.

Anna just stood there as if in shock. Her eyes were big and her mouth was open.

"You all right, Ma'am?" John asked.

"I - - ah - - I don't know," she said as she just looked at him.

"Where were you going?"

"Ah - - to - - ah, the schoolhouse."

"Maybe I should walk you there. Let's get your groceries picked up."

Anna didn't reply, she simply nodded her head. John bent down and gathered the groceries and put them back in the sack. He then stood up. He wanted to reach out and take her arm, but decided that walking next to her was probably the better thing to do.

They started on down the boardwalk. John turned his head and whistled for his horse. The horse walked up behind John and followed him.

Anna didn't say anything. They hadn't gone very far when she turned and looked back at the big man still lying on the ground. She turned back around and walked a little further before she glanced up at John. She wanted to say something, but didn't know what to say to him.

"I wouldn't worry about him," John said. "I'm sure it isn't the first time he's been hit on the head. I doubt he will bother you again."

"You hit him pretty hard," she finally said.

"Yes, Ma'am. I sure did. I wasn't about to let him bother you. It was clear that he scared you, as well it should. He's not a pleasant man."

"Do you know him," Anna asked as she looked up at John's face.

"No, Ma'am. But I know his kind."

Anna turned and looked down the street. She didn't know what to say.

Nothing more was said until they got to the schoolhouse. They stopped out in front and she turned toward him. For a moment, she just looked at him.

"Ah – thank you for escorting me. I want to thank you for coming to my aid."

"You're welcome, Ma'am. I was wondering if you might tell me your name?"

"Yes. It's Anna Bateman."

"It is nice to meet you, Anna," he said as he handed her the sack.

Anna took the sack, turned and went into the schoolhouse. Once inside she turned and looked at John. She watched him as he stepped alongside his horse, put his foot in the stirrup and swung into the saddle. She continued to watch him as he rode away. When he was out of sight, she took her groceries into her living quarters in the back of the schoolhouse.

As she put away her groceries, she found it hard to get John out of her mind. The thought of whether she would see him again passed through her mind. That thought startled her. Since coming to Deadwood, he was the first man she had seen who had caught her interest. She shook her head as if it would get him off her mind, but it didn't help.

John smiled to himself as he rode down the street. When he came to the big man he had struck on the head, he reined up and looked down at him. The big man was sitting on the edge of the boardwalk looking up at John, but he didn't say anything.

"How's your head?" John asked.

"It's felt better," the big man said.

"I think it would be a good idea if you left the schoolteacher alone. You bother her again, and you will have to deal with me."

"I ain't going to bother her again" he said as he reached up and touched the back of his head.

"Good. By the way, you wouldn't happen to know where I might find Jack Storm? He's also known as Indian Jack."

"Yeah. I know him. He's over at the hotel sleeping off a drunk. Why? What's your beef with him?"

"He murdered a storekeeper over near Yankton. He was a friend of mine."

"You out to kill him?"

"Not if I can take him back to stand trial," John said.

"Do you think you can?"

"Yup," John said, then started down the street toward the hotel.

When John got to the hotel, he tied his horse up to the hitching rail and went inside. He walked up to the desk and asked the man behind it what room Indian Jack was in. He made no comment as to why he wanted to talk to Jack.

"He's in room three, but I wouldn't wake him if I was you."

"Why's that."

"He's mighty mean when he first gets up after sleeping off a drunk," the desk clerk said.

"Well, he's had plenty of time to sleep it off. I have business with him."

"Is he expectin' you?"

"I doubt it. I want to surprise him," John said, with a grin.

"He ain't much for surprises."

"I'm sure you're right," John said then turned and headed for the stairs.

John started up the stairs. When he got to the top, he walked down the narrow hall to the door with a three painted on it. He stood back and looked at the door for a minute, then drew his gun and kicked the door open. He quickly stepped into the room and pointed his gun at the man in the bed.

Jack turned over and saw John standing only a few feet from him. He had a gun pointed at him.

"What the hell you think you're doin'," Jack said.

"I'm here to take you back to Yankton to stand trial for the murder of Joseph McAllen. You shot him down in cold blood for only a few dollars," John said.

"You a sheriff or somethin'?"

"No. Just a friend of McAllen. I plan to see that you are hung for what you did."

"I don't think you can get me out of this town. You'll be dead before you reach the town limits," he said with a slight chuckle.

"If anyone tries to stop me, you will be the first to die," John said. "Now get up and get dressed. One wrong move and you will die right here."

John watched Jack as he swung his legs over the side of the bed. As Jack reached for his boots, he dove at John. It turned out to be a big mistake. As he dove, John sidestepped him and laid the barrel of his gun across the back of Jack's neck, and Jack went sprawling out on the floor face down. He was out cold.

John sat down on the edge of the bed and waited for Jack to come around. While he waited, he removed all the bullets from Jack's gun then slipped it back into Jack's holster. He also took a minute to search Jack to make sure that he didn't have any other weapons.

Getting impatient for Jack to come around, John stood up and picked up the pitcher of water on the dresser. He walked over to Jack and poured it over his head. Jack almost instantly woke up. He reached around and touched the back of his neck as he turned over and looked up at John.

"I'll kill you for that," Jack said angrily.

"The wanted poster I have for you says "Dead or Alive". Frankly, at this point, I think you would be a lot less trouble if you were dead. You should be thankful that I want to see you hang. At least that way you will live for a little while longer. Now get dressed. If you try anything, I'll just shoot you and save me the trouble of taking you back."

John stood off to the side and watched Jack very closely while he dressed. As soon as Jack was dressed and had his gun belt on, John opened the door to his room and looked down the hall. The hall was empty.

"We are going down the stairs and out the front door of the hotel. We are going to walk over to the stable and get your horse. Then we are going to ride out of town together."

"Suppose I don't want to go?"

"The next time you decide not to go with me, I'll crack your skull and throw you over your horse and tie you there for the trip all the way back to Yankton. Now get moving," John said as he shoved Jack toward the stairs.

Jack looked at John for a couple of seconds, then turned and started toward the stairs. Although John didn't have his gun in his hand, he made it look like he had his hand on his belt. He was fast with a gun and just having his hand close to his gun was enough to make Jack comply with his request.

They walked through the lobby of the hotel and out onto the boardwalk. Jack turned and started toward the livery stable. John reached out and untied his horse from the hitching rail. The horse followed them along in the street.

As they walked along the boardwalk, John noticed that Jack kept looking around. It was clear Jack was looking for someone to help him. John kept an eye out for anything that didn't look normal. It was not easy to watch every doorway or every space between buildings as they passed by.

They hadn't gotten far when they stepped off the boardwalk. Just as they stepped down, a man across the street yelled at Jack.

"Hey, Jack. Aren't you up a little early?" the man asked as he laughed.

"Yeah," Jack said.

Jack took the chance that John was distracted. He quickly turned and threw a punch at John. It caught John just below his left eye sending him hard up against the building. Jack quickly pressed his attack and hit John several times before backing off. When he backed off, he reached for his gun.

The suddenness of the attack and the hard hitting from Jack had dazed John. Jack went for his gun but when he pulled the trigger the hammer fell on an empty chamber. He looked at the gun and then at John.

John was able to realize that Jack was going to try to kill him and he drew his gun. John was feeling lightheaded. He saw Jack take off around the corner. When John tried to go after him, he fell to the ground and passed out.

Anna had been across the street. She had seen Jack run from between the buildings and head down the street. She wondered what it was that made the man run so fast. As she walked past the space between the buildings, she saw John lying on the ground. She quickly ran to his aid. Anna knelt down next to him.

John was starting to come around, but was still dizzy. Anna helped him to his feet. She had to hold him up.

"I've got to get him," John said.

"You can't. You're hurt."

John looked down at her. She had one arm around his waist and his arm over her shoulder. He realized that he was hurt and would not be able to fight Jack if he were to come back.

"I need a place to hide so I can rest."

"Come with me," Anna said.

Anna took him down between the buildings to the back alley. She helped him along the alley to the backroom of the schoolhouse and took him inside.

Once she was inside the backroom, she laid him down on her bed. She immediately got some water and a washcloth and cleaned the cut on his cheek. When she had done all she could for him, she covered him with a blanket and let him rest. For the rest of the day, Anna spent her time tending to his needs.

It was almost dark when John woke up. He was still sore and had a headache. He turned his head and looked at Anna. She was standing next to her small wood stove making something to eat. She turned around and saw him looking at her. She smiled at him.

"Are you feeling better?"

"Much better. I want to thank you for helping me, but I can't stay here."

"You're not well enough to leave. What would happen if you run into that man again?"

"I can't stay here. What will people say?"

"I don't care what people will say," she said, almost not believing what she had just said.

"You're the schoolteacher. The parents of your students will not like you having a man in your sleeping quarters. You could lose your job here."

Anna didn't say anything more. She thought about what he had said. She knew he was right, but he needed her help. She couldn't just let him go when there was someone looking to probably kill him. Besides, she was finally able to admit to herself that she liked him. She didn't know why, but she did.

"You may be right. I could lose my job, but I can always get a new one somewhere else."

"I don't want to be the reason you lose your job."

"You will lose your life if you leave now," she countered.

John knew she was right. He was in no shape to take on Jack. There was little else he could do but stay and rest.

"I have made a stew. Do you think you could eat a little," Anna asked.

"Yes, Ma'am."

He watched her as she spooned the stew into a bowl. She took it over to him and set it on the table next to the bed. She leaned over him and put a couple of pillows behind him, then gave him the bowl. She got a bowl of stew for herself, then sat down beside the bed and ate with him. They ate in silence, each one worried about the other.

After they finished eating and Anna had cleaned up the dishes, she sat down beside him to talk. Anna found him to be a very interesting man. It was obvious to her that he was fairly well educated.

John found out that she was from St. Louis, and had gone to school there. She had been offered the job as the schoolteacher by a business man in Deadwood who wanted the children of Deadwood to be educated at least in the basics.

It was late before they blew out the lantern. John fell asleep in her bed while Anna slept in a chair.

When morning came, John was up and out of Anna's room before dawn. The last thing he wanted was for her to lose her job because she took care of him. He had left a note on the pillow of Anna's bed before he left to find Indian Jack. The note read – "I left so no one would know I spent the night in your room. I am going to finish what I started out to do. When I am done, I will come back to you. John."

John started out for the hotel. He figured that Jack would be sleeping off a drunk. He had gotten no more than a few houses from the schoolhouse when he heard a scream coming from somewhere behind him. He turned and looked back toward the schoolhouse. There was a horse tied out in front.

John was sure that it was Anna who had screamed. He started to run back to the schoolhouse. He approached the building carefully. John moved alongside the building and peeked in a window. He could see Jack and Anna inside. Jack had a hold on Anna's arm and was yelling at her.

"Where is he?" he yelled. "You'll tell me, or I'll beat it out of you."

"I don't know where he is," Anna cried.

"I know he spent the night here with you."

John went over to the door of the schoolhouse and very carefully opened it. Jack had his back to him and didn't see John step inside the school.

"Drop the gun and let her go," John demanded.

Jack quickly swung around, pulling Anna in front of him. He had his gun pointed at Anna.

"You drop the gun, or I'll shoot her."

"If you are stupid enough to shoot a woman, it will be the last person you shoot. And I will be the last person you see alive," John said as he held his pistol pointed right at Jack's head. "Even if you kill her and kill me, there isn't a man in this town who won't be hunting you down to hang you from the nearest tree for shooting a woman. Even the sheriff won't be able to protect you."

"I've already shot one woman," he said with a grin.

John knew Anna was scared. He could see her trembling. He had to do something before she panicked and got someone killed.

There was also the fact that there would be children coming to school shortly. There was little time to end the situation. It was at that moment he heard the sounds of children coming toward the school.

Jack must have heard the children, too. He looked toward the door. When he did, the end of his pistol barrel moved away from Anna's head.

John didn't hesitate one second. He pulled the trigger. The loud noise of the gun going off filled the room along with gun smoke. He had no more than fired when he ran to Anna and grabbed her by the arm to pull her away from Jack as he fell to the floor. Anna turned into John and buried her face in his shoulder.

Anna still had her face on John's shoulder, and he still had his arms around her when the sheriff came into the school. He took a look around and saw Jack lying on the floor. It was clear that Jack was dead. The sheriff looked at John and walked over to him.

"I told you that your wanted poster was no good here. You are under arrest for murder."

That statement by the sheriff brought Anna's head off John's shoulder.

"You can't arrest him. He saved my life from that man. He had a gun pointed at my head," she screamed.

The sheriff looked at her then at John. He knew there was more to it than Jack attacking the schoolteacher. He also knew that if he arrested John, he would end up looking like a fool. No one in the town thought much of Jack anyway. He was well known for being a bully and a mean man who liked to show everyone just how mean he really was.

On the other hand, Anna was well known by the town people, too. But she was well respected and thought of as a good person. If it came to a trial, Anna's word would get him off. There was only one thing for the sheriff to do, that was to let John go.

"Okay. I think you should call off school for the day while we get someone over here to clean up the place."

"Thank you, Sheriff," Anna said.

As soon as everyone had cleared out, Anna walked with John to the livery stable. John rented a buggy. They took the buggy to a nice quiet place that Anna knew about. They spent a good part of the day on a blanket eating lunch and talking.

Two months later, Anna and John got married. John took the reward money and bought a small ranch outside of Deadwood. Together they raised a family.

JEFFERSON JONES

Jefferson Jones was a hunter and trapper who made his living off the land. Anyone that knew him would call him a Mountain Man. He had spent the past two years trapping for beaver and other animals in and around the Black Hills. He had enough pelts from beaver, coyotes, wolves and bears that it was time to take the long journey to the trading post at Fort Pierre on the Missouri River. He would travel downstream along Elk Creek to the Cheyenne River. From there he would follow the Cheyenne River to where it flowed into the Missouri River, then on down the Missouri River to Fort Pierre.

Travel was slow, but the weather had been fairly comfortable. His travel time was shortened on some days due to heavy afternoon and evening thunderstorms. Other days he could travel until it was almost dark. There were many dangers along the way, but not just from Indians, the weather and animals. There were some who would like to have Jefferson's pelts. He had to keep a careful watch at all times.

The days soon turned into weeks. The horses fed on the grasses that grew along the banks of the rivers. Jefferson would stop regularly so the horses could drink from the rivers. He would camp under the large cottonwood trees that grew along the river's edge. The cottonwood trees would provide him with branches to hang his shelter on when the weather was not good. They would also provide him with firewood for cooking.

As the summer grew hot, Jefferson came to where the Cheyenne River flowed into the Missouri River. Staying on the west bank of the Missouri, he headed south to Fort Pierre. He was not sure how far it was, but it really didn't matter. He had pelts to trade and he needed to go wherever he could trade them.

Jefferson had not traveled very far along the Missouri River when he came upon a small camp. There were four men at the camp. They were sitting around a campfire when Jefferson came around the bend. He stopped suddenly and looked at the men.

There was something about these men that caused him to become vigilant and cautious.

It was probably the fact that they were sitting around a fire in the middle of the day that caused Jefferson to become cautious. That alone was reason enough for him to be suspicious of them. Any man sitting around in the middle of the day was either sick, lazy or up to no good, at least to Jefferson's way of thinking. None of the men looked sick or injured. He thought about going a different way, but it was too late. He had already been seen.

One of the men saw Jefferson and smiled. He leaned over and said something to the man next to him. They then looked back at Jefferson and smiled.

"Come in," the man said pleasantly as he motioned for Jefferson to come closer. "Sit down and have a cup of coffee."

Jefferson was hesitant, but what choice did he have? They were on the only trail in the area he knew, and it was too difficult to go around them. There was also the fact that he had been seen. Jefferson cautiously moved closer to their camp, stopping just long enough to tie his horses to a nearby tree. He then took his cup from his pack and walked over to the campfire.

"Help yourself to the coffee," one of the men said.

Jefferson leaned down, picked up the coffee pot from the fire and poured some into his cup. He then set the coffeepot back on the fire, but didn't sit down.

"Sit a spell," another one said.

Jefferson sat down, then looked at each of the men. The one who had invited him to sit at their fire was a short, rather stocky man with broad shoulders. He had the look of a frontiersman, but Jefferson thought he looked like he might be a bit on the lazy side. He might have thought that way because the man was lying against a log, and he looked unkempt. The man had a rather large potbelly, his hair was uncombed and his beard was dirty with tobacco stain in it. His clothes were as dirty as the man himself. He carried a rather long sharp knife on his belt, and there was a rifle leaning against the log he was reclining against.

"Where ya headed?" the one who had told him to help himself to coffee asked.

Jefferson didn't like the looks of that man any better. He was a little taller than the others, and had shifty eyes. He was also slimmer than the others and seemed a bit nervous. He had a thick mustache that was stained with tobacco juice. He was wearing a coonskin cap. His hair hung out from under it and looked tangled and dirty. He looked as if he had not had a bath in a month, maybe more. He also had a rifle leaning against a tree only about four feet away. The thing that troubled Jefferson the most was he kept eyeing Jefferson's horses and the load they carried.

"I'm going to Fort Pierre."

"Tradin' furs, are ya?" the third man asked.

The third man was as dirty looking as the others. He was sitting on a log with a cup of coffee that he was holding in both hands. His hands looked like they hadn't done a day's work in years.

However, it was the forth man that seemed to bother Jefferson the most. He hadn't said a single word. He just sat there looking at Jefferson with cold dark eyes. He was a tall man with dirty blond hair. His beard was short and his teeth yellowed with tobacco stains. The way he looked at Jefferson made him think it would not take much for the man to become violent. He just plain looked mean.

"Yeah," Jefferson answered as he turned his attention to the man who had spoken to him.

"Looks like ya had a good season."

"I did okay."

Jefferson was a bit nervous. There were too many guns and knives very close to the men. He had a feeling that these men would do him harm and take his pelts, if they thought for one minute they could get away with it without getting hurt in the process.

Jefferson decided it would be best if he could get away from them without making them suspicious, or without upsetting them. He would try to leave in such a way as to avoid making them think that he didn't trust them. Jefferson was sure they already knew he didn't trust them. Jefferson finished his coffee and stood up. He shook the few drops of coffee from his cup.

"Thanks for the coffee. I think I should get a move on."

"What's your hurry? The tradin' post ain't goin' nowheres," the short stocky man said with a grin.

"I've got a long way to go," Jefferson said with a smile.

Jefferson turned and walked back to his horses. He didn't like having his back to them. He held his hand on the pistol in his belt while listening to make sure they didn't try to sneak up behind him or go for their guns. He heard no movement on the part of the four men. He was sure they had seen the gun he carried in his belt as well as the knife.

As he untied his lead horse, he watched the four men. They remained at the fire and just watched him as he swung up on the back of his lead horse. He noticed that they watched as each of his horses walked by their camp.

With the way they were looking over his horses, Jefferson was sure they were appraising the value of the load each horse was carrying.

Jefferson had not seen any horses around the camp, nor had he seen a canoe or any other kind of boat. He thought they might be on foot. If that was the case, he would move a little faster. He knew that just because he had not see nor heard their horses, it didn't mean they were on foot. He felt that they were too lazy to walk. They probably had horses somewhere close by.

As soon as he was around the next bend where he could no longer be seen by them, he nudged his horses along a little faster. He wanted to put as much distance between him and the men as he could before dark. Jefferson kept up the faster pace for several miles before he let the horses slow down to an easy walk. Jefferson may have slowed his pace a bit, but he kept his horses moving.

It was getting on toward dark when he found a place where he thought he could stop for the night. It was off the trail a little ways, and it would be easy to hide his horses from anyone on the trail. After unpacking his horses and staking his bundles of furs, he hobbled the horses in a small clearing to eat and sleep. He set up his camp close to the edge of the woods so he could duck back into the woods if he should be attacked. He decided that he would do without a fire, and eat hardtack and jerky with a little water. It would be too easy for an enemy to find him if he had a fire. Even if it couldn't be seen, a fire could be smelled for some distance.

Jefferson ate his meal then leaned back against a tree where he could look over the small clearing where his horses grazed and slept. It had been a long day and he was tired, but he sat under the tree and listened to the night. As the night went on, he found himself dozing off, then waking with a start. He couldn't seem to keep his eyes open. He finally drifted off to sleep.

* * * *

Jefferson had dozed off, but woke suddenly when he felt something wrap around his chest. It pulled him hard against the tree he had been leaning against. His eyes flew open. Jefferson quickly realized that someone had wrapped a rope around him and was pulling him tightly against the tree. He struggled for only a moment before he realized it was of little use. He would have to wait and hope that his moment would come, then he would strike back and strike back hard.

"Thought you could get rid of us, did ya?" the short stocky man said to him. "Sam, take his guns and knife."

The one who had said nothing at their camp, reached over and took Jefferson's knife then looked it over. He smiled as he looked at it before holding it up for the others to see. It was obvious that Sam thought it was a good knife.

"That's a nice knife, Sam. You can keep it if'n ya want. He ain't goin' ta have no more use fur it, no how."

Sam smiled, then slipped the knife in his belt. He turned around and took Jefferson's rifle and the pistol as well. Jefferson could have kicked himself for falling asleep. He should have kept going, even if it meant traveling all night, but it was too late to worry about what he thought he should have done. Instead, it was time to figure out what he could do to escape, and get his pelts back.

"Hey, Jessup. You should see these," the taller of the four men said. "These here are some of the best furs I've seen in a long time."

"I had a feelin' they'd be nice, Lester."

"Billy, tie him tight. I want ta take a look at them furs."

"Okay, Jessup," Billy said.

Jefferson could feel the rope being tied tighter around him, but he also noticed that Billy was not paying very close attention to what he was doing. He seemed to be more interested in Jefferson's pelts than in tying a proper knot. Jefferson could see that the knot Billy was tying was not a very good one. It was clear Billy didn't know how to tie a knot that would hold fast. Jefferson was also well aware of the fact that they had failed to search him for any other weapons.

"Leave them furs bundled, Lester," Jessup said. "We'll load 'um back on his horses and take them, too."

"But won't they get us for horse stealin'?" Billy asked. "We could get hung for that."

"Look at them horses, stupid. Them's Indian ponies. Ain't nobody goin' ta think twice about 'um. Besides, by the time they find his body, ain't nobody goin' ta be able ta recognize him no how. Now let's get outa here."

"What about him?" Lester asked as he pointed at Jefferson.

"Lester, you and Billy get them horses loaded up," Jessup said. "Sam, you wait here 'til we've been gone for a little while, then you can take your time killin' him."

Sam didn't say a word. All he did was nod his head and smile, and occasionally made a grunting sound.

While three of the thieves loaded the bundles of pelts onto the horses, Sam watched impatiently. He could hardly wait to get at Jefferson.

Jefferson worked to loosen the rope while Sam watched and waited for the others to get the pelts loaded onto the horses. The knot

Billy had tied allowed the rope to slip a little when Jefferson moved against the rope. Each time it slipped, it gave Jefferson a little more room to move. When he finally had enough room to move his arms, he leaned forward while watching Sam. When he was close enough, he reached inside his high-top moccasins and pulled out a small knife. He concealed the knife in his hands, then waited for his opportunity.

Once the pelts had been loaded on the horses, Jessup walked over to Jefferson. He knelt down next to him with Sam standing close by watching.

"Sam can't talk none. Ya see, an Injin cut his tongue out after he screamed at the Injin for scalpin' his folks. Now he's goin' ta scalp ya, then he's goin' ta cut your throat," Jessup said with a grin. "By the time anybody finds ya, there won't be nothin' left of ya but your bones."

Jefferson didn't say anything. Jefferson wanted more than anything to kill Jessup, but if he did it now he would certainly be killed by the others. He could wait for a little while.

He would wait until the others had gone and he would have only Sam to deal with. Once they were out of sight, he would kill Sam.

"Got nothin' ta say?" Jessup asked, then laughed.

Again Jefferson said nothing. He simply looked at Jessup. There was nothing to say.

Jessup stood up, looked at Jefferson for a moment and then started walking away while Sam stood by Jefferson and watched them leave. Sam was too busy watching the others to pay any attention to Jefferson. Keeping an eye on Sam, Jefferson cut the rope, then held the ends of the rope together in his hands so Sam would not be able to see that the rope had been cut. Jefferson then prepared himself for what he had to do.

Sam began to smile to himself as he watched the other three thieves leave. He was sure he was going to enjoy what he had planned for Jefferson.

As soon as three of the thieves were out of sight, Sam turned and looked down at Jefferson. Sam held the knife up in front of

Jefferson's face giving him a chance to look at it. He wanted to make sure Jefferson would know that he would be scalped and then killed with is own knife. Jefferson waited.

When Sam knelt down beside Jefferson, he reached out and took hold of Jefferson by his hair. He started to lean forward to scalp Jefferson. In one swift move, Jefferson swung his arms free and stabbed Sam just under his ribs. Sam's eyes got big with surprise and his mouth flew open as if to scream, but he only made a growling noise. The knife fell from Sam's hand. When Sam looked down at Jefferson, Jefferson stabbed him again then rolled to the side as he pushed Sam away.

Jefferson quickly got out from under the rope and stood up. He looked down at Sam. He was lying there on the ground with his eyes open. Sam was dead, but the look of terror and surprise remained on his face.

He quickly grabbed up his knife and tucked it into his belt. Jefferson then took Sam's gun along with his ball and cap pouch and powder horn. They had left behind Jefferson's pouch of hardtack and jerky, and his bedroll.

Jefferson rolled everything he could into his bedroll and put it over his shoulder like a bandoleer.

After taking back his own pistol from Sam, he started off at a run to go after the thieves and his pelts. Jefferson grabbed up his rifle on his way by the tree it was leaning against. He wasn't sure how he would get his pelts back, but he was now armed and would get them back or die trying.

Jefferson suddenly stopped. He slowly turned and looked back at where he had camped. He had suddenly realized the other three thieves had left riding on horses that were not his. That could only mean they had left a horse somewhere back in the woods for Sam. Without a horse, he might not be able to catch up with them before they got to a trading post and sold his pelts.

Jefferson began slowly walking back toward where his camp had been. He moved very quietly in the hope of hearing something that would tell him where Sam's horse might be hidden. By the time he got back to where his camp had been he had heard nothing. He stood silently while looking around. Just as he was going to start his search of the area, he heard what sounded like a horse chomping on grass. He smiled to himself and started walking toward the sound. He found a horse that was saddled and ready to ride tied to a tree. The horse had been grazing on the grass around the base of the tree.

He untied the horse, put his foot in the stirrup, swung his leg over the saddle and sat down. Jefferson had never used an American style saddle before but found it very comfortable. Having been raised in England, he was only familiar with the smaller and lighter English saddle.

Jefferson nudged the horse in its sides and started down the trail after the thieves. He set a gait that would cover a lot of ground without wearing out the horse too quickly. He needed to catch up to them before they could get to Fort Pierre and sell his pelts. Once they were sold, he would not be able to get them back. He would not be able to prove that they had been stolen from him.

Jefferson kept an eye on the trail to make sure the thieves didn't cut off the trail somewhere along the way. He paid close attention to what was ahead of him. Jefferson wanted to be sure he saw them before they saw him. He knew he was outnumbered and would need every advantage he could get, no matter how little it might be.

The trail made a sweeping turn as it followed the bend in the river. Off in the distance, he thought he could see several horses through the trees. They were walking along the trail as if out for a stroll.

Jefferson pulled up and looked through the trees. Now all he had to do was figure out how to get his horses and pelts back.

While trying to figure out how he was going to get his pelts and horses back, the horses stopped. Jefferson wondered what they were doing. The thieves appeared to be discussing something. He wasn't sure what was going on until he saw one of the riders swing his horse around and start back up the trail.

Jefferson realized they must have started to wonder what happened to Sam. If Sam had killed Jefferson like he should have, Sam would have caught up with them by now. He had to do something very quickly or the rider would see him. He looked around and saw a large cottonwood tree that hung over the trail. The branches were full of leaves making it hard to see if there was anything or anybody in the tree.

Jefferson jumped down off the horse and quickly tied it behind some bushes where it could not be seen. He then ran over to the tree and climbed up into it as fast as he could. Once in the tree, Jefferson quickly moved out onto the branch that hung over the trail. Gripping his rifle with one hand and holding on to a branch with the other, he waited.

Through the leaves, Jefferson could not see who was riding so fast, but he was ready. Holding onto the branch tightly with one hand, he swung the rifle down as the rider passed under the branch. The rider saw the rifle coming at him a split second before it hit him. He had not been quick enough to duck the rifle as it came at him. The butt of Jefferson's rifle caught the rider on the side of his head and knocked him off his horse. The horse continued to run down the trail a little ways without its rider.

Jefferson scrambled out of the tree and ran toward the rider. He got to the rider just as he was trying to stand up. Jefferson hit him again with the butt of his rifle, knocking him out. He turned the rider over and found it to be the younger of the thieves, Billy. Since he was out cold, Jefferson dragged him off the trail and down into a shallow ditch. Jefferson quickly tied Billy to a tree and put a gag in his mouth to prevent him from warning the others if he should come around.

Leaving his horse tied to the tree, Jefferson began to work his way along the edge of the trail toward the thieves. Keeping close to the bushes along the trail, he was able to sneak up to within thirty feet of the two remaining thieves without being seen. He hunkered down behind a bush and watched them as he tried to decide what to do next. He could hear Jessup and Lester talking.

"Ya don't think that trapper got loose and killt Sam, do ya?" Lester asked.

"Nay. Sam would have killed him. He was tied pretty good," Jessup said.

"Then why do ya think he's takin' so long?"

"Ya know Sam. He enjoys his work. Remember what he did ta the last trapper we took furs from?" he said as he laughed.

"Yeah. Ya could hear him scream for miles," Lester laughed.

Jefferson had heard enough. He raised his rifle and pointed it at Jessup then slowly cocked it.

"Don't either of you move unless you want to die," Jefferson said in a clear firm voice.

Hearing the sound of Jefferson's voice confused the two men for a few seconds. Suddenly, Jessup dove into the bushes alongside the trail. Jefferson had no time to shoot at him.

Lester was confused and looked around as if he didn't know what to do. When he started to move, Jefferson shot Lester hitting him in the leg. Lester fell down in the middle of the trail, and screamed with pain as he laid on the trail grabbing his leg. The horses shied and trotted down the trail a little ways.

Jefferson quickly drew his pistol from his belt and waited. He listened to see if Jessup was going to try to fight back. Being careful to keep his pistol where he could reach it quickly, he began reloading his rifle. As soon as his rifle was ready, Jefferson tucked his pistol back in his belt and called out to Jessup.

"You ready to give me back my pelts?"

"I wondered if'n it was you. At first I thought it was someone else tryin' ta steal our furs," Jessup replied.

"They are not your furs."

"They is as long as I have 'um."

"Well, I guess they won't be yours much longer."

"That remains ta be seen."

Just then there was the sound of a gun being fired and a lead ball crashing through the branches of a tree just to Jefferson's left.

"That was close, weren't it?" Jessup said with a laugh.

Jefferson didn't say anything. He had seen where the shot had come from. It was time to move, but he had to do it very quietly.

"You'll never sneak up on me. I've got good cover here. I can wait ya out 'til Billy gets back."

"Jessup, help me," Lester called out in pain as he looked toward Jessup.

Jefferson could see Lester and where he was looking. It gave him a good idea where Jessup was hiding. Slowly and carefully, Jefferson pulled back away from his position behind the bushes. He worked his way back along the trail. Jefferson kept in the bushes so he could not be seen by Lester.

When he was far enough back around the curve in the trail, he cut across the trail to the other side then ran in among the trees. Jefferson quickly began working his way back to where Jessup was hiding.

It wasn't long before Jefferson could see Jessup hiding behind a large rock. He was still looking toward the bushes where Jefferson had been. He could see that Jessup was getting a little nervous. He had not heard or seen Jefferson for several minutes, although to Jessup it probably seemed more like hours.

Jefferson took careful aim at Jessup. He was about to tell him to give it up when Jessup turned and spotted him. Jessup started to swing his rifle around, but he was not quick enough. Jefferson pulled the trigger. His gun fired and the lead ball caught Jessup square in the chest. Jessup rose up and fell backwards over the rock. He lay in the grass behind the large rock with his eyes looking upward at the sky. The front of his shirt was covered with his blood.

Jefferson reloaded his rifle before he stood up and walked to the trail. He turned and walked back up the trail to where he had left Sam's horse. He mounted up then went on down the trail to retrieve Billy's horse. He then retrieved the horses that Jessup and Lester had been riding as well as his own horses.

After Jefferson gathered up all the horses, he secured them so they would not run off. He then walked back down the trail and got

Billy. Billy was awake, but had a terrible headache. He marched Billy to where Lester was lying on the trail, then tied him to a tree.

Once they were secure, Jefferson gathered up all the weapons and added them to the packs on his horses. When he had everything secured on the packhorses, he walked back to Lester and Billy.

"Jessup and Sam are both dead," Jefferson said. "The two of you are the only ones left. By all rights, I should hang both of you for stealing my horses and my pelts."

"Oh, God, please. Don't hang me," Billy cried.

"Why shouldn't I? You knew what you were doing."

"Please, mister," Lester pleaded as he looked up at Jefferson.

Jefferson looked at the wretched souls. He knew they would have taken his life in a heartbeat, and two of them had even tried. Although Jefferson had no reason to show them mercy, he couldn't help but think that killing them when they were so helpless was not the right thing to do. He had never killed a man for the sake of killing. He certainly had never killed anyone except to protect his life or his property.

"I will spare your miserable lives on two conditions," Jefferson said as the looked at them. "The first is I get to keep your horses."

"You can't leave us here without horses," Lester said.

"Since you put it that way, I'll just hang you now and take them anyway. I think I have earned them."

"No. You can have them," Billy said.

"Lester?" Jefferson asked as he looked at him.

"You can take them," he said relenting, not really having a choice.

"You said two conditions." Billy said, getting a harsh look from Lester.

"The second is that you leave this part of the country forever. If I see you again, I will shoot you on sight with no warning."

"We'll leave," Billy said then looked to Lester for his response.

"Yeah. We'll leave," Lester agreed reluctantly.

"Good. I will leave you one horse. Back along the trail is a trail that goes south. I suggest you take it. I hear Texas is nice this time of year. It's a lot nicer there than it is for you here. If you choose to follow me, I will kill you both. Do you understand?"

Billy looked at Lester, then turned and looked at Jefferson. He then nodded that they understood.

"What about our guns?" Billy asked. "We'll need them for protection."

"I will leave you one gun with a small amount of powder and shot around the next corner. I'll leave it with a horse. If you are smart, you will take my advice and leave this area as quickly as possible. And Billy, clean and dress Lester's wound as soon as you can. If it gets infected, he will most likely die."

"Yes, sir."

With that settled, Jefferson walked to where he had tied the horses. He picked out one of the horses, tied one rifle to the saddle and put a few rounds of shot and one powder horn in the saddle bags. He then walked over to the other horses. He mounted the one he had been riding, took the reins of the lead horse and headed on down the trail. When he got well around the corner, he stopped long enough to tie the horse with the rifle on its saddle to a tree, then went on his way. He had gained three horses with saddles and saddle bags, three rifles, four pistols and several knives. He considered them payment for all the trouble he had gone through to recover his furs.

Jefferson rode on down the trail leaving the thieves behind to make their way as best they could. It may not have been the right thing to do, but it pretty well assured Jefferson that they would not be following him anytime soon. He would keep an eye out for them, just the same. He hoped they would take his advice and head south.

It was another three days before he arrived at the Trading Post at Fort Pierre on the Missouri River. He traded his pelts for the things he would need to return to the Black Hills for another year of hunting and trapping. Once he had his supplies packed on the backs of his horses, he left to return to the Wilderness.

WANTED DEAD OR ALIVE

The wind was blowing out of the northwest across the open prairie. It was a cold wind that made a body feel cold to the bone. It wasn't snowing, but it sure felt like it could start at any minute. Winter would soon be upon the land.

The big dapple gray horse plodded across the land with his head hanging down. The rider, Max Pierson, had his sheepskin coat wrapped tightly around him, and the collar pulled up around his neck and over his ears. With all the dust blowing, it was hard for Max to see where he was going.

Max had been following four men from one town to the next for several weeks. Up until the windstorm, he had been slowly gaining on the men. He could only hope that the men he was after would hold up somewhere.

Although he couldn't see the sun, Max could see that it was slowly growing darker. He would have to find a place to hold up for the night. Just as he was thinking it was about time he should be coming to the small town of Fairpoint on the prairie of the Dakota Territory, he thought he saw a light off to his right. He turned his horse toward the light.

It wasn't long and he found himself in front of a saloon in Fairpoint. He stepped out of the saddle and looked around while tying his horse to the hitching rail. He then stepped up onto the boardwalk in the front of the saloon. The street was empty. He could see several lights in the windows of buildings nearby. He turned and walked into the saloon.

Once inside the saloon, Max stopped and looked around. There were eight people, counting the barkeep, in the saloon. The barkeep was standing behind the bar looking at Max when he came through the door.

"Pretty nasty weather to be out there. Come on in and sit a spell," the barkeep said.

"Can you tell me where the livery stable is? I'd like to put up my horse first."

"Sure. It's down at the end of the street. Chester should be there, but if he ain't just put your horse in a stall. He'll be by here 'for long."

"Thanks," Max said then left the saloon to take care of his horse.

When Max got to the stable, there was no one there. He opened the door and led his horse inside. He found an empty stall and led his horse into it. He took a rag and wiped out the horse's nostrils then took his saddle off. He then wiped his horse down and fed him.

As soon as his horse was taken care of, Max took a look in the other stalls in the barn. He quickly recognized the four horses that were in the stalls. They were the horses the men he was after had been riding.

Just then there was a noise behind him. Max quickly drew his gun as he spun around sharply to see who was there. A stocky, strong looking man stood there with the fear of death on his face. He quickly put his hands in the air as he looked at the gun that was pointed at him.

"Who are you?" Max asked.

"I own this stable," he said nervously.

"Are you Chester?"

"Yeah," he replied.

"You can put your hands down. The barkeep at the saloon said I could put my horse up here," Max said as he put his gun in his holster.

"Yeah, that's fine."

"How much do I owe you?"

"Four bits if you used my feed."

"Here," Max said as he handed the man four bits.

"Are you running from the law?" Chester asked.

"No. What makes you think that?"

"You're pretty fast with that gun."

"I'm looking for the four men who own those horses," Max said as he pointed to the stalls.

"There's only three of 'um now. They are over at the saloon. What did they do?"

"They robbed a bank over near Fort Pierre. They're wanted for killing a kid and a woman who just happened to be in the way. They also killed two people in the bank."

"You a lawman?"

"No," Max said. "What happened to the fourth man?"

"He come in with 'um, but he was all shot up. He died a few minutes after they got here."

"What's the condition of the other three?"

"I think the tall skinny one might be injured. He's keeping his right arm tucked in close to his side. The other two don't look like they're hurt at all," Chester said.

"Thanks for the information. I would like it if you wouldn't say anything about me to them."

"No problem. I don't like men who kill women and children."

"Thanks," Max said, then turned and walked out of the stable.

It wasn't long before Max was standing outside the saloon. He was looking in the window. He could see the three men standing at the bar. Chester might have been right. The tall skinny one seemed to use his left hand for everything. He also kept his right arm tucked up against his side as if he was protecting it. Max also noticed that his gun was on his right side, a good indication that he was right handed. He was sure he was the one they called "Stick" because he was so tall and skinny. He was also known to be good with a gun.

Max took a few minutes to look at the other two men. One he knew as Grant. He was a fairly big, stocky man. He looked like he might be pretty strong. He had broad shoulders and his arms filled out the sleeves of his coat pretty well. His hands looked big, too.

The third man at the bar was about average build. Max was sure he was known as "Skinner". There was nothing special about him except for the long, very sharp looking knife he carried in his belt.

Max walked into the saloon. He had only taken a couple of steps into the saloon when the barkeep spoke to him. When the barkeep spoke, two of the three men at the bar turned to see who had come in. Stick was the only one who didn't turn to see who came in.

"What can I get for you?" the barkeep asked.

"Can I get a cup of coffee and something to eat?" Max asked.

"Sure can. This is the only place to get something eat in this town," the barkeep said with a grin. "Sit down and I'll whip you up a steak and potatoes."

"That would be great."

"Coffee pot's on the stove."

Max walked over to the end of the bar and picked up a cup. He then went to the stove to fill the cup. Once he had his coffee, he looked at the others in the saloon while walking to a table close to the wall.

Sitting at a table on the other side of the room were two men. One of them was playing a card game while the other was leaning back in a chair with his feet up on the chair next to him. The two men looked like cowboys who were just sitting out the storm.

After sitting down with his cup of coffee to wait for his dinner, he took time to look at the two other people in the saloon. One was a young man sitting at a table in the corner. He was nursing a beer while talking to the young woman sitting next to him.

The young woman looked like she might work in the saloon. She was blond with her hair hanging down to her shoulders in ringlets. She was wearing a dress with a fairly short skirt and a low cut neckline.

Max turned his attention to the three at the bar just as the barkeep came out of the back with a plate with a steak and fried potatoes on it. He set the plate down in front of Max with a knife and fork.

"Anything else I can get for ya," the barkeep asked.

"No. This will be fine."

The barkeep turned and went around behind the bar. Max watched the people in the saloon while he ate his dinner. It seemed to be a fairly quiet evening. It was as if everyone was just waiting out the storm.

As Max casually watched what was going on in the saloon, he noticed a dark spot on the edge of Stick's shirt just above the belt. It was almost hidden by Stick's arm that he held close to his side. He began to think Stick was using his arm to protect his wound from further injury, or to keep pressure on the wound to keep it from bleeding.

Max's attention was drawn to Grant as he leaned closer to Stick. He couldn't hear what he was saying, but as he leaned away from Stick, Stick turned his head and looked at Max. Max had to wonder if Grant had figured out who he was. If he had, it would make things harder for Max.

Max waited until Stick and Grant were no longer looking toward him. As soon as he was sure he was not being watched, he slipped his extra gun out from under his coat and held it under the table in his left hand. There was little doubt that things could get a little dicey if they figured out who he was. With his right hand, he picked up his coffee cup and took a sip while keeping an eye on the three at the bar. Max slowly pushed back away from the table in an effort to give himself a little more room to move.

Things started to happen very fast. Suddenly, Grant swung around as he drew his gun. At the same time, Skinner started to draw his gun and Stick moved further away from the other two.

Max pushed over the table as he shot at Grant with his spare pistol while drawing his sidearm. His first shot caught Grant in the chest and knocked him back against the bar. Max's second shot clipped Skinner on his left cheek spinning him around.

Stick drew his gun from his holster on his right side with his left hand. It made getting off a quick shot difficult. As a result, Max was able to get off a shot from his sidearm that caught Stick just above his belt buckle. That shot put Stick down for keeps.

Max felt a sharp burning pain in his left arm as another shot was fired. He turned as he started to fall. He fired another shot at Skinner that caught him in the left side of his chest.

The gun fight took only a matter of a few seconds. Grant was dead when he hit the floor, Skinner was mortally wounded and Stick was gut shot and would die before morning. Max had a gunshot wound to his left arm, but it was not life threatening.

The young woman in the bar helped dress Max's wound. He spent a couple of days in

Fairpoint before he left the small town and returned to Fort Pierre to collect the bounty on the three he caught in Fairpoint in the Dakota Territory.